# STARFALL

A DURGA SYSTEM NOVELLA

## JESSIE KWAK

# STARFALL

## A DURGA SYSTEM NOVELLA

JESSIE KWAK

*For my parents,*
*who raised me strong and curious.*

# 1

## STARLA

G ravity here is crushing.

Starla Dusai switches gingerly from side to back to sitting, the terrible mass of this planet making it hard to breathe, making her joints and bones ache, her heart race at the slightest movement.

Not that she has much opportunity to move.

The cell she's in is about two paces wide and just long enough for the cot — which is not long enough for Starla. At fifteen, she's already shot past her Indira-born parents by a full head, growth spurts set free by the low gravity of Silk Station.

She's tried to sleep the last three nights with legs crooked up and spine curled forward, but the ache in her knees wakes her, the ache in whichever side is being rammed by this planet's gravity through the thin mattress.

The ache in her heart of not knowing if anyone else is still alive.

Cot, sink, toilet. Harsh yellow overhead lights that call out sickly undertones in her pale-colored skin. The walls are featureless but for what looks like a speaker and a camera in the ceiling opposite the cot, where she can't reach. Useless to her, anyway.

Food is dispensed automatically through a slot at what seems like regular times. The lights dim and rise. A cleaning bot scurries through every afternoon and then slips back into its pocket door. On the second day, Starla tried to catch it, but it shocked her so badly the muscles in her hands twitched for what felt like an hour. She lets it do its job in peace now.

The air smells sharp and scorched, like a recycler system gone over-hot and baking its seals. The temperature is uncomfortably warm.

It's what she's always imagined desert-hot New Sarjun would smell like.

Because she's on New Sarjun.

She has to be.

She's in an Alliance prison colony on New Sarjun.

There's no place else she could possibly be.

---

At the end of the third day, guards.

A man and a woman, wearing the same uniform as the Alliance soldiers who'd transported her from Silk Station. They slip through the door, come at her with outstretched hands and careful quiet steps like they're trying to corner a wild animal and they're not sure it won't bite. The man says something to his partner, his pudgy lips mashing the words into meaningless shapes.

They don't bother trying to speak to her.

Starla pushes herself into the corner of the cot, feet digging into the mattress. She's snarling as they pounce, drag her to her feet — she's panting with the effort of moving on this stupid, stupid planet — and wrench her arms backwards into cuffs. They push her through the door. She's barefoot.

Starla tries to stay calm, but for as badly as she has wanted to leave the cell over the last three days, now the metallic, vibrating hallways and branching corridors close in on her. She cranes her neck to see down the corridors they pass and is rewarded with a shove between the shoulder blades.

The two wrestle her through hallways, keying regularly through double-thickness glass doors to enter less secure — or more secure? Starla doesn't know — areas of the prison. Into a dingy metal room, bigger than her cell, a single metal table bolted to the floor, a bench on one side, a chair on the other. They fold her kicking and struggling and panting onto the bench, uncuff her, and slam her hands into new restraints on the table before she even realizes she had a brief moment of freedom.

Job done. The two leave.

Starla twists, cranes her neck to see the door they left through, trying to learn anything she can about this new prison.

Brushed aluminum walls and a floor scuffed with shoe rubber — some of the marks scraping high up the wall as though someone had been testing the strength of it, or kicking out in anger. The walls are battered, with dents and dings that catch the harsh light and pool it into tiny craters. The room stinks of something acrid, a mix of cleaning solvent and welding fumes that seems to be cycling through the air vents.

Starla coughs.

She's waiting only a moment before two women enter. One's short, even for planetborn, with a blunt gray bob and glasses, wearing a plain purple dress suit. The other's tall and thin, with a square jaw and thick black hair cut close to her scalp. She wears an Indiran Alliance uniform. They remind her of something, a split second of recognition that fades the more Starla tries to grasp at it.

The short woman wrinkles her nose and says something to the tall one, too fast for Starla to catch.

"Hi Starla," the short woman says then, speaking and signing. "My name is Hali." She spells it out, then makes her hand into an *H* and taps it against her left shoulder. "This is Lieutenant Mahr." Mahr doesn't get a name sign.

Starla lifts her chin a touch, but makes no show that she's understood. The short woman, Hali, frowns at her.

"She's a child," Hali says to the Alliance woman, Mahr. She's speaking more clearly now than when she first entered the room. Starla stares at her lips, greedy for information. "You can't keep her like this. There are laws."

The lieutenant shrugs. "Figure out what she knows," she says — or, Starla thinks she says. The lieutenant's lips barely move, her scowl permanently carved into her dry, angry mouth.

Hali turns back to Starla, speaking and signing again. "Have they treated you well?"

Starla frowns. What is she supposed to answer to that? Everything's fine, thanks for asking? The amenities could be a bit more posh, but they're serviceable?

She raises a hand to sign something rude, but she's cuffed to the table.

Her hand comes up short with a jerk.

"We can't communicate if she's restrained," Hali says to Mahr.

If Mahr replies, Starla can't tell. The lieutenant turns to knock on the door, looks like she shouts something through it, and one of the original guards returns with leg restraints, locking Starla to the crossbar of the bench before releasing her hands. "Thank you," Hali tells him. He ignores her.

Hali sits in the chair across from Starla; Mahr leans against the wall with arms crossed, one hand resting on the stunner in her hip holster. Hali sees this and frowns. "She's a child," she says again. Mahr just raises an eyebrow.

Starla sits with hands folded. Trying to look like a child, whatever children look like on Indira. She's heard her entire life, from newcomers to Silk Station, from people born on either planet — Indira or New Sarjun — that she and her asteroid-born cousins look years ahead of their age because of their height. On some, like Mona, it looks graceful. On Starla it just looks boyish and scrappy. One of the uncles told her that once. She thinks he meant it as a compliment.

A stab of panic pierces Starla's heart.

She tries not to worry about her cousins. About Mona. About Auntie Faye. About her parents. She saw escape pods, shooting like torpedoes; she saw ships peeling away from docking bays and flashing out of view before the Alliance missiles tore through the station and set Starla's home blazing bright as Durga herself.

1, 4, 9, 16, 25 . . .

Starla forces herself through multiplications to redirect her thoughts.

She's missed something: Hali signing to her. Starla furrows her brow, and Hali repeats herself. "I'm here to decide what to do with you. Do you understand?"

Starla finally nods. She's found that if she refuses to respond at all, some people write off communication for good. This might be her only chance to get answers.

"*Good.*" The woman's still speaking aloud while her hands dance, probably for Mahr's benefit. "Do you know where you are?"

Starla considers. Is the woman gauging her knowledge of geography, or her intelligence in general? Probably both. "Prison," Starla signs. "New Sarjun."

Hali frowns at that last sign, and Starla fingerspells it. She can't remember the standard USL sign for New Sarjun — she and Mona had their own slang for so many things.

"Yes," says Hali. "That's right. You're under Alliance protection."

"My parents: what happened?" Starla leaves the last sign hanging in the air a moment before resting her hands back on the table.

Hali looks at Mahr, who's apparently said something to her — Starla sees only the last few syllables slicing out of Mahr's sneering lips. "She's asking about her parents," Hali says. Mahr just shakes her head.

"We'll get to that," Hali says and signs to Starla. "But for now I have some questions. Can you tell me about life on Silk Station? Were you taken care of there?"

Starla wrinkles her nose. "It was home," she signs, confused. Was she taken care of there? What the hell was that supposed to mean?

"Who raised you?"

Starla glances from Hali to Mahr, who is watching her coldly. What are these questions?

"My parents raised me," Starla signs. "Where are they?"

Hali ignores her question. "I'm confused. Did your parents take you with them on their raids? On the *Nanshe*?"

"Of course not," Starla signs. She'd wanted to go for years, but they hadn't let her. Not until this year, until her fifteenth birthday, when they'd finally agreed she could start training as crew. If not for that, she wouldn't have been on the *Nanshe* when the Alliance attacked Silk Station. Wouldn't have —

Hali is waving to get her attention. "Then who raised you when they were gone?"

Starla shrugs. What, did this woman want a list? Any number of aunts, uncles, older cousins, station mechanics, and cooks had done the job.

Starla and the other children had stalked Silk Station, hurtling through the corridors as if propelled by rockets, chasing after older cousins in the peculiar game they played in the figure-eight hallway near the bioregenerative gardens, screaming and reversing directions on a toe, arms flinging out to correct over-exuberant spins in the low gravity. They were legion, underfoot, existing continuously on the verge between play and being snatched up by one of the station crew and given a chore.

Dinners were the same chaos, a gaggle of children descending on the commissary at any hour, whenever they were hungry. School was TUTOR, an AI that came preloaded with courses from Hypatia Educational Facilities Corporation that students could work through at will, with full knowledge that their progress data was being reported to the aunts and uncles. Curfew was a word from the novels she downloaded from TUTOR.

Who had raised her?

"Whoever was around," Starla signs.

"Whoever was around," Hali says, and she and Mahr share a look full of meaning that Starla can't decipher. "You're very thin," she says and signs to Starla. "Did they feed you well?"

What the hell did that mean?

Starla glares at her. "Where are my parents?"

"We're just trying to understand your life," Hali says, hands fluid and defensive. "You're on the edge of what the Alliance considers a child. Your parents chose to become criminals, but you had no choice. You've had a hard life. Do you understand?"

Starla feels a chill. Raj and Lasadi Dusai chose to live life on the fringes, managing their glorious and infamous empire from an asteroid station hidden deep in the debris of Durga's Belt. Starla Dusai, on the other hand, could tell a sob story about being beaten and neglected and starved at the hands of her horrible pirate parents, and win a free ticket into the open arms of the Indiran Alliance. A free ticket into the society her parents had fled years ago.

"Where are my parents?" Starla snarls the words on stiff, angry fingers.

Hali looks sad. "I don't think she's ready to talk yet," she says to Mahr.

Mahr knocks on the door and the two guards come back in, hands and stunners raised to subdue her.

"Where are — "

Starla gets only those words out before her hands are grabbed, her arms cuffed, her ribs slammed into the hard metal edge of the table.

They drag her back to her cell.

# 2

## JAANTZEN

Willem Jaantzen is fifteen breaths away from pulling the trigger. He's counting them: One, two . . . The bulk of the pistol feels like a living thing nestled against his chest.

Ahead, Mayor Thala Coeur of Bulari is shaking hands with the Cormoran ambassador, welcoming him to New Sarjun's capital city, her teeth gleaming white in that picture-perfect smile as she turns to the cameras. She's changed little these three years, rust-colored skin still glowing and taut, hair plaited into a cascade of tiny braids — not bound brash with gold as she'd once done when she controlled only the Nova neighborhood, but more classically styled these days. Appealing to all her voters.

Three, four.

It's hot today, baking. Mirages shimmer up from the sidewalks, and all through the crowd fans are snapping open and shut, misters floating above, wafting down cooler breezes on their turbine gusts.

Jaantzen glances up at one of the misters for a split second, catches the gold glint of the surveillance cam in the center. Wonders if this is one of the Bulari Police Department's, or one of Toshiyo's. He can't tell the difference, and he doesn't care. That's why he hires the sharpest people he can find — to ensure that moments like this go off without any hitches.

To say that Willem Jaantzen has spent three years dreaming of this particular moment would be misleading. He's thorough, not excessive. Dedicated, not single-minded. He's spent three years preparing, yes.

Three years obsessing, no.

Ahead, Coeur exchanges a joke with the ambassador, claps him too heavily on the shoulder. The man flinches, and Jaantzen feels a hint of pride for his city, almost. Coeur may be wearing the veneer of civility, but the fierce woman who styled herself Blackheart when she ran Bulari's most powerful crime organization is still there beneath the surface.

Good.

Jaantzen gets no pleasure from slaughtering sheep.

Jaantzen's earpiece crackles and he hears Toshiyo's telltale clearing of the throat. "What is it," he snaps.

"Boss. Julieta Yang's calling."

Jaantzen blinks. Twice.

Breathes.

"Have her speak with Manu." That's the plan, not Toshiyo calling in to interrupt him after she's given him the all clear. Manu Juric is the executor of all that comes after this moment.

"Boss, I tried that."

Not a surprise. In Bulari's underground, Julieta Yang is one of his fiercest rivals and oldest friends, yet they rarely speak about business. If she had a petty business matter to discuss, she'd have had one of her daughters call.

No. Julieta Yang called because she, Julieta, has something to say to him, Willem. Right now.

Coeur turns for another photo op, holding her million-mark smile only slightly longer than the camera before turning towards the entrance to the Indiran Alliance Embassy. Her security guards scan the crowds, their eyes skimming over Jaantzen.

Nine, ten.

"Boss?"

Right now, Jaantzen should be making his peace. He clenches his jaw and tries to blend in, another face in the crowd. He'll look into Coeur's eyes in the moment, but if she recognizes him too early, the game's over.

And she will recognize him. She will know it's Willem Jaantzen who finally got his revenge.

Eleven, twelve.

He wants to ignore this call, ignore Toshiyo and get on with his plan. Since Toshiyo gave him the go-ahead he's seen only one face in his mind's eye: Tae's.

He wonders if Coeur ever thinks about Tae and his children.

He wonders if she ever holds her own family close in the dark and marvels that their fragile little lives have lasted this long in the bloody wars of Bulari's underworld.

"Boss?"

It's time, but his hand isn't reaching for the gun.

"How long is the mayor's speech slated to be?" he murmurs.

Toshiyo's relief is evident in her voice. "Thirty minutes. They'll be leaving out the Commerce Street entrance."

Coeur offers her arm to the ambassador, and they both walk up the stairs.

Willem Jaantzen melts back into the crowd.

"What in sweet damnation does Yang want?"

---

Jaantzen finds a corner table in a cafe he trusts and Toshiyo patches the call through to his earpiece. Julieta Yang won't answer a video call, only voice. She's convinced video calls are easier to track, no matter what anyone else tells her. One of the mister drones has followed him from the plaza; it dips its wings twice, Toshiyo's signal.

Willem Jaantzen doesn't relax.

"Madame Yang," Jaantzen says, waving away the waiter, the owner's son. The boy hovers, watchful yet discreet and visibly nervous. He's not used to being alone around Jaantzen. "How may I help you today?"

Julieta Yang's voice is cool and aloof, gone papery around the edges with age in the years since they first met. He'd been a fool child just getting started in the game, and she'd come herself to deal with him for poaching on her territory. All these years later, and she can still make him feel like a fool child with the right tone.

"My people have intercepted troubling news about mutual friends of ours," she says. Never for the small talk, Julieta goes straight to the point — "Life's too short to pretend to care how someone is doing," she'd told him once.

Jaantzen doesn't ask; waits for her to tell him. He's sweating more than usual — he can smell himself through the expensive suit and the nice cologne: the sharp bite of adrenaline. His body had prepared itself for the inevitable hail of bullets and is having trouble adjusting to the fact he's still alive.

"The Alliance attacked Silk Station three days ago," Julieta says. "By all accounts, they destroyed it."

An echoey silence in Jaantzen's head; the restaurant seems hushed. There but for the grace of God go we all, one fiery explosion away from having no family, one volley of torpedoes away from having one's entire organization, everyone one cares for and protects, completely destroyed. He signals to the owner's son for a glass of wine.

"Any survivors?" he asks once he's sure the horror won't color his voice.

"Yes," she says. "There was enough warning for some of the family to flee before the Alliance began firing. Reports are still coming in."

"Raj and Lasadi?"

"The *Nanshe* was apparently mobile when the Alliance attacked. It was boarded and prisoners were taken. We haven't been able to learn whether Raj and Lasadi were among them." A pause. "I was hoping you could do that. It's more your expertise."

"I can connect you with Toshiyo — "

"I don't need your surveillance team," Julieta snaps. "My surveillance is the best. I need your political connections."

Jaantzen checks the time on his comm, takes a sip of the wine. He has ten minutes to get back in place by his count; as if on cue, Toshiyo sends an update: SHE'S WRAPPING UP. 10MIN TO EXIT. YOU GOOD BOSS?

Jaantzen's not good.

Raj and Lasadi Dusai have taken care of themselves and their family for decades. If the Alliance got them this time, it's because they stretched past their limits, picked the wrong pocket, slit the wrong throat.

They'd nearly done it seventeen years ago when they tried to turn over a ship containing one Willem Jaantzen. Fortunately, the result of that encounter had been lifelong friendship.

Julieta Yang's business would be taking a dip with the loss of the Dusais and their steady supply of pirated goods, but he knew that wasn't the only reason she was upset. Raj and Lasadi Dusai, once you'd met them, were infectious. Their business partners often found themselves unexpectedly becoming friends.

If Raj and Lasadi planned right, their family — their daughter; he thinks of her with a pang and moves on — will be taken care of. Like Jaantzen's people will be.

Jaantzen has taken care of everything. His legitimate businesses are all shielded from backlash through layers of red tape, his illegitimate ones dissolved and the assets put into a fund to be distributed by Manu Juric, who will ensure that everyone is comfortable during the transition.

Right now, Jaantzen should be thinking about Tae and his children. Preparing to see them, should that be his option in the ever-mysterious afterlife.

He doesn't need to be thinking about the Dusais.

"I'm in the middle of something right now," he says. He's not telling Julieta what. He doesn't need her blessing — or her chiding.

A sharp breath on the other end of the call. "Ah, yes. I heard what you've planned for today, and I think it idiotic."

He doesn't ask how she knows, and in seven minutes it won't matter. He drains the glass of wine and authorizes a hundred-mark transfer to more than cover the bill. He stands, nods to the owner's boy. "I thought you'd appreciate the chance to soak up some of my territory," he tells Yang.

"Those idiots in the Sendera Dathúil would get there before me, you know that, Willem. Things are good in Bulari now. Balanced. Don't toss the lot of us into the churn."

"That's not my concern, Julieta. I'm taking care of my people. You can take care of yourself, Raj and Lasadi can take care of themselves, and the Sendera can go to hell. I'm paying my own debts today."

The mister is trailing behind him, veering from hanging plant basket to hanging plant basket like a working drone would. His comm buzzes: Toshiyo. 5 MIN BOSS. Ahead, he can hear the noise of the crowd; he starts to slip into the outskirts, blending in.

Julieta Yang is still in his ear, but he's already gone, scanning the plaza to check the guards, check the misters. He's working his way to the front of the crowd.

"We have learned one thing," Julieta says, and his attention snaps back to the conversation, caught by her tone. She's been holding back a card, and she's ready to play. He tenses. "We know they've captured the daughter."

Jaantzen doesn't answer, but he's doing the math. How old is the girl now? He hasn't seen her since she was just starting to walk, when Raj and Lasadi brought her with them on one of their many trips planetside. She'd been about the same age as his daughter Sora had been when —

Now she'd be fourteen — no, fifteen.

Now the Alliance has the girl, will they treat her as a child, or as an adult, a traitor?

"Raj and Lasadi made you godfather, didn't they?" Julieta asks, but it isn't a question, and again he doesn't bother wondering how she knows. Julieta Yang's specialty is expensive luxury goods and even more expensive information — both of dubious origin.

"She's being held in Redrock Prison," Julieta says, like she's telling him tomorrow's weather forecast. "Here. On-planet," like there might be other Redrock Prisons. He can almost hear her examining her cuticles with feigned disinterest.

Two minutes.

"You know people who could help, don't you," says Julieta, and for a moment he thinks he hears worry in her voice. "There's nothing I'll be able to do about it."

The last time he saw the girl, she was all gangly limbs and graceless toddler exuberance, that same glorious joy and innocence as his Sora and Mikal, yet so different in her fierce desire to break free from her parents' orbit.

There's a flurry of activity in the guards by the door; the moment is here. He hasn't seen Starla in years, but he's seen Raj, he's gotten updates on his goddaughter, he's made renewed promises over business dinners to take care of her if anything ever happened to Raj and Lasadi.

Ahead of him, Coeur is walking out, flashing that smile and a palm-out wave to the crowds below her. Her gaze dances over him, and the pistol in its holster burns hot and fierce. He buttons his coat.

"Dammit, Julieta," he says.

"Let me know what you find out," she says. "I'll help where I can."

# 3

## STARLA

Starla's back in her cell, door slammed and lights flicked off to pitch black — even the dim lights that had glowed through the other nights. A spike of fear in her chest. Starla wonders if lights-out is punishment for not telling Hali and Mahr what they wanted to hear. Sensory deprivation to make her afraid.

1, 4, 9, 16 . . . She counts her squares like Deyva always told her to do, whenever she was angry at a mechanical problem whose solution was eluding her. She gets as high as 17 times 17 before she feels the panic subsiding.

Starla lies back on her cot with knees bent.

It's just darkness. It's not a punishment, it's just a reminder of the deep black, of that inky, starry night she's been plucked from. She belongs among the stars, not here.

She realizes her eyes are still open, and closes them.

She remembers.

Starla's hands were clumsy in the EVA suit she'd stolen from her mother, but she'd been practicing making her gestures bigger so that Mona could read her signs even through the unsubtle suit. Of course, they wouldn't always have visual communication, so Starla had reprogrammed the heads-up display on her mother's helmet to show her what Mona was typing. She had programmed a glove to recognize what she was fingerspelling and transmit that to Mona.

Starla carefully removed the right glove from her mother's suit, replacing it with the one she had modded herself. She stared at the lower left corner of her screen, waiting for the glove to patch into the system.

GLOVE_TEST_3 DETECTED, blinked the screen. Starla suppressed her delight. It was working.

She glanced over at Mona, who looked nervous. "No backup system," Mona signed. Starla nodded. She knew. But this was a trial run, just to make sure she could communicate. Eventually, they would get a backup system in place. She certainly wouldn't be comfortable relying only on her modded glove to pass messages back, not if she ever got to go out on the skin of the *Nanshe*.

Starla slowly began to fingerspell the alphabet, watching as each letter appeared in the lower corner of her screen. *A – B – C* . . . She glanced over at Mona, who was staring at her comm. Mona nodded, signing the letters she saw back to Starla.

Starla felt a thrill of excitement.

Should work like a charm.

"Ready," signed Starla, and Mona grimaced nervously.

Her scaredy-cat cousin was as ready as she'd ever be.

Starla's mother's suit was snug, but Starla had been nervous about stealing a suit from a taller cousin. Her mother's would just have to do.

Mona glanced up at the ceiling in that gesture Starla had learned to recognize: an announcement was coming over the intercom. For some reason she couldn't fathom, everyone looked to the direction the sound was coming from like it helped them hear it better.

As expected, Starla felt her comm buzzing in her pocket — three short jabs. She couldn't reach it, not geared up as she was, and she hadn't had time to patch her incoming messages into her mother's helmet where she could read them.

Starla waved to get Mona's attention. "What is it? Comm in pocket," she signed.

"Shuttle docking in the bay right next door," Mona signed back. "Maybe we should wait until tomorrow."

"No."

No way was she getting this close without testing the glove outside. After years of waiting, Starla's parents had finally agreed to let her join one of their training runs with the new recruits. She would show them that she was ready, that she was resourceful. That she should join their crew permanently.

Starla punched the button for the airlock, and the door slowly began to open.

She felt a tap on her shoulder — the sensation muffled through the suit — and turned to see Mona shaking her head. "We know the glove works," she signed. "Try tomorrow?"

Starla shook her head again. "Mom's already going to yell at me," Starla signed. "Might as well earn it."

Mona looked resigned. "I'll get yelled at, too."

"Tell them I made you do it."

"That doesn't work anymore."

Despite her nerves, Starla grinned. They had been getting into trouble for years together, and Mona had almost always been able to talk herself out of trouble by saying she was just watching out for Starla. It never bothered Starla — even on the times Mona had come along willingly, Starla had always been the instigator.

They were as opposite as could be. Mona was curious about books and history, spending hours on her own with TUTOR learning about the harsh early days of settlement on Indira, about life on the *Ark Matsya*, about old Earth. Starla had put in the required hours with TUTOR, trying to get the AI to teach her what she was really curious about: electronics, programming, mechanics, weaponry. She soon found that TUTOR's curriculum was annoyingly theoretical, and although she continued to work her way through the calculus and physics courses just so the AI wouldn't ping her mother that she was skipping lessons, Starla began spending more time down in the mechanics bay learning about the daily operation of the station and getting her hands dirty in its wired guts.

"I'm going," she signed. Mona's shoulders slumped. "Now."

Fear, delicious and electric, thrilled through her as she stepped through the airlock door. Starla took a deep breath. She could feel the pressure change as the door slid shut, and she deliberately turned away from the window separating her from Mona.

Behind her were the familiar corridors of Silk Station. Behind her were generations of a tangled family tree and many friendly transplants — all too quick to step in and help out whenever she had trouble with something.

In front of her was the black, glittering with stars. She took a step forward, tentative, though the outer airlock wasn't even open — the thick glass still seemed too thin — and startled when the broad, scarred side of a shuttle lumbered across her view. The shuttle that was docking in the bay next door. Right. She took another deep breath.

A message from Mona popped up on her screen. *You OK?*

Starla almost turned around to give her a thumbs-up, but she had to break herself from relying on visual communication. She made a fist and signed yes, instead, and to her delight the glove captured the movement. *Y-E-S.* Starla beamed.

She had never been outside the station in an EVA suit, but she'd done the drills, and she'd read about it. She'd watched TUTOR's instructional videos and gotten one of her older cousins, Amit, to talk her through it one day when he was in the middle of a passionate anti-Alliance diatribe and too distracted to wonder why she was asking.

She waited until the shuttle was past the window before starting the sequence Amit had given her. Next time she would have to figure out how to patch her comm into the helmet — she felt naked without her connection to the rest of the station — but that wouldn't be hard.

O-P-N-N-I-N-G-N-O-W, she fingerspelled, and the glove translated each letter. One typo. Not bad, but still some fine-tuning to do.

CHECK BELT CLIP, Mona typed back.

Starla sighed and checked her tether, then she did turn back to give her cousin a thumbs-up and a grin. Mona looked terrified.

Starla hit the button.

She could feel it, the sensation of the vacuum a subtle thing yet phenomenally alien. Starla self-consciously checked the belt clip again, feeling the reassuring tension of it tethering her to the station. She wouldn't be going anywhere. She would be fine.

Starla stood at the edge of the airlock, gripping the handrail on the left side as she stared out into the expanse. Blackness, washed with stars and studded by the ever-shifting vista of the asteroids that made up Durga's Belt.

It was the same view she'd seen every day of her life, but today there was no glass between her and the void.

She realized the lower left corner of her screen was blinking, annoyed. O-O-O-O-O

She let go of the handrail and the Os stopped.

There was a bug she would have to fix.

WHATS WRONG, came Mona's response, predictably.

N-O-T-H-I-N-G-S-T-U-P-I-D-G-L-O-V-N

Starla frowned at the glove, annoyed.

She could still feel the thrumming of the station around her, the minute vibrations and shifts, the way it shivered from time to time like a living creature. It was more intense at the core, but here, out at the edge? Silk Station felt like a distant memory.

Starla fought the wild urge to let herself float free towards the heavens.

She could feel the gravity of the station still, feel its life and energy through her feet. The place she'd known her whole life, the energy she'd experienced for fifteen years. The same old people with their same old stories and complaints and dramas.

The black expanse beckoned her with its tantalizing unknowns, and damned if Starla was going to stand on the edge of it and not taste it.

GOOD TEST RUN. COME BACK IN?

N-O-T-Y-E-T

Starla hadn't gotten this far just to open up an airlock and stand at the threshold.

Starla stepped out.

---

It's still dark in her cell, but Starla is smiling, the memory of floating soothing the ache in her bones, the memory of Mona soothing the pain in her heart.

And the scent that had lingered on her suit when she'd reentered Silk Station, that faint, metallic scent like the fumes from a welder, or the antifreeze Deyva used to flush the systems. The smell of space.

Starla can still remember it, if she tries.

She'll fly again.

Alliance be damned.

# 4

## JAANTZEN

Jaantzen steeples his fingers in the glow of the screens, trying to ignore the rat's nest of tangled cables and gadgets and drifts of unlabeled data sticks littered over the tables, keeping his attention on the data streaming across the central monitor.

"How much longer?" Jaantzen asks.

It makes his skin crawl to be down here in the clutter and chaos, which Toshiyo navigates with deftness. She plucks data sticks out of their disorderly piles without looking, mutters epithets beneath her breath at each flicker and stall of her computers. She slaps a monitor on the side and Jaantzen winces.

It does no good to remind her who is paying for all this equipment she so haphazardly scatters throughout her lair, and Jaantzen has stopped doing so. He's hired people at the top of their game and given them what they need to do their jobs. And he's learned the best thing to do is sit back and stay out of it.

Besides, buying out Toshiyo's indenture was a costlier investment than any of these pieces of equipment, and since he's given her — and all his people — the choice to stay or go, the smartest thing he can do is make sure she's happy working for him.

She's been almost drunk with relief since he returned to the office this morning, her words tumbling over each other and attention flung recklessly throughout the room. Jaantzen finds it charming to know just how much she would have missed him.

Manu Juric is happy to see him, too, bustling about the office like a mother hen to make sure Jaantzen has everything he might need. Jaantzen isn't sure what Manu would have done had Jaantzen gone through with his plan to kill Coeur; Jaantzen would have left him enough money that he wouldn't have to work, but Jaantzen can't imagine the man sitting back and doing nothing.

Toshiyo's black-lacquered nails clatter against the keyboard, and after a long moment, Jaantzen begins to suspect she's forgotten he asked her a question.

"Ms. Ravi?" She looks up him and blinks, her glossy black ponytail catching the light of the screen. "How long?"

"Oh. Five minutes," she says, turning back to her keyboard.

Five minutes. It seems like an eternity, one in which he can only sit and curse Julieta Yang. She was right about there being nothing Toshiyo could do for her — Julieta's information was the best. Which is why he doesn't believe that she doesn't know whether Raj and Lasadi were among those captured from the *Nanshe*. She'd known about the girl. Why wouldn't she know about the parents?

Jaantzen finishes the dregs of his green tea, grimacing — he's trying to quit coffee today. His doctor, Gia, has given him any dozen number of things he should quit if he wants to live a good long life, which Jaantzen has been ignoring given his circumstances with Coeur.

But now that this chance — so perfectly choreographed — has been destroyed, he's thinking again. "You wanna live to kill that bitch, you gotta start skipping dessert, boss" — those had been Gia's exact words. The little luxuries — cigars, red meat (as rare as that was on New Sarjun), anything else that raises blood pressure — were to be plucked one by one out of his arsenal of foods until only blandness remained.

Rice and beans. Even just the words conjure up memories of the tasteless, watery, pale brown glop that was the staple of every homeless shelter and food bank he'd eaten at as a child. Bland food has long been linked in his mind with those starving years. At least the Willem Jaantzen of today can afford any spice in the galaxy, if he likes.

At mealtimes, this may be a consolation. Right now, he just wishes he could buy a few minutes' speed out of Toshiyo's servers.

"You want, I can let you know when I have an answer," Toshiyo says, not looking away from her screens. Her drawl is pure rural New Sarjun; he picked up her indenture from a mining conglomerate out in Ruby Basin after hearing stories about a young ops tech with an uncanny ability to glance at a spreadsheet and pinpoint a motherlode. Streaming data pools in her black eyes.

"Am I bothering you?"

She spares him a frown. "No," she says, too quick.

"Then what is it?"

Deep sigh, her thin shoulder climbing and dropping. "I'm not supposed to stress you out," she says. A quick sideways glance, flash of green catching in her irises. "Gia's orders."

Jaantzen's doctor is enlisting help from his staff.

Lovely.

"I promise I won't die of a heart attack on your watch, Ms. Ravi."

She doesn't look convinced. Gia is formidable, but Jaantzen likes to think of himself as more so — and he'll be even more so as soon as he loses a bit of the girth he's allowed to accumulate around his waistline since Tae —

Willem Jaantzen shifts in his chair. "How much longer?"

Toshiyo's attention snaps back to the monitors, her mouth quirks into a smile. "Got it." But it's another full minute of tap-tap-typing until she sits back. Jaantzen feels like he's about to explode.

"The lists for Redrock Prison show one Starla Dusai," she says. "Maximum security wing, isolation cell."

Jaantzen relaxes at that. Isolation means she won't be at the mercy of the worst of the worst to be found in maximum security. It may not be comfortable for the girl, but at least she's not in with the general population.

"And her parents?" he asks.

Toshiyo frowns at her screen. "They were picked up from the *Nanshe*, but they haven't been recorded as entering any Alliance prison on New Sarjun."

"So, they're being kept elsewhere, they've been checked in under alternate names, or they're dead," says Jaantzen. Toshiyo nods slowly. "Find me every suspicious name in the timeframe," he says.

He's not ready to entertain the possibility that they're dead. Not when their daughter is waiting for them to come for her.

Jaantzen stands, almost bumping his head on a low-hanging shelf. He's got nearly half a meter on Toshiyo. "And find me someone in that prison who can be bought or convinced."

"Yeah, boss."

Jaantzen can't quite turn away; he's been dancing on the edge of his last request. Toshiyo senses him there, fingers going still. She glances over her shoulder. "Boss?"

"And find out Mayor Coeur's schedule for the next month."

She doesn't look at him. Cracks a knuckle on each hand. "You got it," she finally says.

She's typing away, back in her own world. Jaantzen stands in the doorway, watching. He wonders what she would have done if he'd killed Coeur. Gone to work for Julieta, maybe? Or pivoted straight and narrow to work for some corporation indenture-free? He likes to think she would have found some place to be happy and live a more normal life. He makes a note to ensure her employment with someone trustworthy before he takes his next chance at Coeur; he'd been remiss in this, last time.

His stomach growls. It's time to follow his next lead.

---

Seventeen years ago, Willem Jaantzen took to the skies to protect his cargo from the scourge of the shipping lanes: the *Nanshe*. Part favor to himself, part favor to Julieta Yang, who had agreed to fund the trip and had sent one of her daughters along to negotiate her own terms with the infamous pirates.

Jaantzen mostly remembers being miserable. It's the only time he's left New Sarjun, and he never intends to again.

But face to face with the famously rakish captain Raj Dusai, negotiations ended with guns at each other's heads, the tension shattered when Raj broke into his huge belly laugh and tossed away his weapon, inviting Jaantzen and his crew to share in a meal of New Manilan delicacies obtained from an Alliance cruiser.

Raj and Lasadi primarily preyed on Alliance ships, a habit Jaantzen warned them about repeatedly. They claimed it wasn't political, but Jaantzen knew better — the Dusais hated the Alliance with all the fire of Durga herself. And that fire burned them in the end.

Even so, Jaantzen can understand. In the early days of his operations, Jaantzen had been full of anger and rage at those whose politics had thrown him to the dogs. He flaunted himself at police, took pride in destroying petty politicians' lives. The stronger he got, the less care he took.

But as he grew older, he began to understand the value of highly functional relationships with strategic people in power — even if he didn't agree with their politics.

Particularly if they were people with whom he shared a certain civic pride, and a desire to keep New Sarjun free from the Alliance's yoke.

People like Youssef Tabari.

---

Jaantzen walks to the Arcadia, something that will make Gia proud though it gives his security fits. His organization is back to normal operations now, which means Manu Juric can once again insist on setting guards even this deep within Jaantzen's territory.

The Arcadia is a classy establishment just outside the tourist district — a place Youssef Tabari certainly can't afford on his government salary. It's a good way to keep the balance ever so slightly in Jaantzen's favor. A good number of the staff owe Jaantzen their loyalty, plus, the hostess keeps a pistol in her stand. She's a crack shot; he's seen her use it.

Jaantzen's men clear him to enter the restaurant; the hostess shows him to his favorite booth near the kitchen. On the other side of the pass-through window, the head chef raises a hand in greeting.

Jaantzen orders a bottle of wine as Youssef walks through the door, then stands to greet his old friend with a hug.

"I have to get back to work after this," says Youssef predictably as Jaantzen pours the wine, but he picks up the offered glass anyway. As he always does.

It's small talk as they order, Jaantzen going through the motions of putting Youssef at ease. Tedious, but Youssef is a prize associate. Over the years he's become very highly placed in the Trade Commission of New Sarjun, on track to the top job of commissioner within another election cycle or two. As a man who specializes in imports and exports, Jaantzen will do what it takes to have Youssef on his side.

Jaantzen clinks glasses again after the waitress brings out their meal: chickpeas and dumplings swimming in a spice-laden sauce. It's not on the menu — Jaantzen prefers the surprise, lets the head chef choose.

"I hope you don't mind me treating you to dinner today," he says. "I have something that I need to ask you." Youssef leans back, spoon hovering over his plate. Wary. "What do you know about the Dusai family?"

He can see Youssef judging his answer, deciding how to proceed.

"Surely you heard Silk Station was destroyed a few days ago," Jaantzen says, prompting.

Youssef blinks. "That was highly classified," he says. "I barely have clearance to be told myself."

"The Alliance is coy with their information," Jaantzen says smoothly. The Indiran Alliance and their withholding of information involving New Sarjun is a constant thorn in Youssef's side, and Jaantzen prods that thorn gently, a reminder that they're both playing for the same team, regardless of which side of the law they're currently on.

It's the thing Jaantzen likes most about New Sarjun. A deft manipulation of political tensions can erase many a criminal record. Hell, it had gotten Coeur elected mayor.

"The Alliance didn't need to tell us anything," Youssef says. "Durga's Belt isn't New Sarjunian space." He chews, slowly. "The Dusais were suppliers of yours, weren't they?"

"Not suppliers," Jaantzen says. "But we had an amicable arrangement."

"I can't say many but you will be sad to see them gone," says Youssef.

"Perhaps not. But I do have certain obligations that need to be fulfilled. I know their daughter is being held at Redrock Prison. I need to find out what happened to Raj and Lasadi."

"I'd assume they'd have been taken to prison, as well."

"Then I'll need to call in a favor. How quickly can you get me credentials to fly in to Redrock?"

Youssef's jaw tenses. "I can't do that."

"Yes, you can, old friend," Jaantzen says. Youssef can do any number of things; Jaantzen has seen it. "I need to get the girl out of prison. Possibly her parents, too."

"Why would I help you with that?"

"Because without Silk Station, without the *Nanshe*, the Dusais aren't a threat to New Sarjunian commerce, any more than I am." Youssef's eyebrows rise at that. "And the girl's only a child. Fifteen. The Alliance can't hold her for her parents' crimes."

"They can hold her for whatever they want," says Youssef. "They're the Alliance."

Jaantzen tilts his head, spoon halfway to his mouth. "Isn't this our planet?"

"I'm not starting a political war for you," Youssef says.

"I'm not asking for a war. But I'd guess others might feel as we do about the Alliance kidnapping children — particularly when they're keeping them in maximum security prisons on *our* planet. I'd guess there might be a few key people who find this something to be irked about. I just want to reward them for doing the right thing."

Youssef's fingertips tap at the table. "How much?" he asks.

"I think you're familiar with how much I value assistance of this magnitude — and how much I value information," answers Jaantzen. "Particularly something like the classified Alliance records of the attack on the *Nanshe*."

Youssef nods slowly. "I'll see what I can do." He mops his plate with naan. "And fast. If they decide the girl's involved with the OIC, they can do whatever they want with her."

Jaantzen frowns at that. "The Dusais weren't OIC."

"It doesn't matter. If the Alliance decides they need to get rid of someone, all they have to do is prove that person is reasonably likely to be OIC."

"Even a child?"

"Old friend, she's not a child to the Alliance," Youssef says. "They've locked away younger than her, if they thought they were terrorists."

"Then let's work fast," Jaantzen says, dropping his napkin to his plate and standing to offer his hand. Youssef's smile is wary, his hand slightly clammy. Nervous. Jaantzen lets his smile grow more generous.

His comm buzzes as Youssef is walking out the door: Toshiyo.

FOUND A CONTACT. ALLIANCE OFFICER NAMED XIMENA NAYAR. BUT YOU'RE NOT GOING TO BE HAPPY ABOUT THIS ONE.

Jaantzen frowns at the name, trying to remember if he's heard it before. *I'LL BE BACK SHORTLY,* he types. *WITH LUNCH.*

He sits back down and signals the waitress for a to-go order of chickpeas and dumplings. He feels suddenly very tired.

OIC.

No matter what happened to Raj and Lasadi, he won't be able to fool himself into thinking their daughter's age will guarantee her safety in Alliance custody.

# 5

## STARLA

Starla's been wrestled into the interrogation room again, feet restrained, hands free. She shifts on the metal bench, back aching from holding her spine straight in this gravity without a backrest. She slouches. Straightens. Rolls her shoulders.

After what seems like an hour, the Interrogation Twins return: Hali and Mahr.

Mahr looks like she sleeps standing up in her uniform so it — and she — won't wrinkle. Hali's in green today, with a fake flower pinned on her lapel. She's obviously not military. Some civilian contractor flown in to help with the deaf girl. Starla wonders if there's more call for that sort of thing on backwater New Sarjun than on Indira.

She's remembered now what they remind her of: it's an old children's vid she and Mona used to watch, with a family of clowns living aboard a spaceship. Mahr and Hali are the two moms, one stiff and militaristic, one round and matronly. Starla can't remember the names of the characters, but it gives her satisfaction to have recalled this much.

"How are you today?" asks Hali, signing and speaking for Mahr's benefit.

"Water," Starla signs back.

It's been the most pressing thing on her mind. The heat of this stupid planet is sucking her dry, her knuckles cracking and lips flaked to bleeding; she can't stop picking at them.

"Can we get her some water?" Hali asks Mahr, who says something out the door. The water comes in a flimsy plastic bottle that wrinkles under the slightest touch. Starla takes it with both hands to keep it from spilling.

She thinks of Deyva, who had boasted he could make a weapon from anything and had tried to teach her to do the same.

Can't make this piece of garbage bottle into a weapon, that's for sure.

She doesn't look at Hali until she's done drinking, even though she can tell the woman's trying to get her attention. Starla sets the bottle aside, nearly empty, and wipes her dry lips on the back of her hand.

"We have some other questions today," Hali signs and says when Starla finally makes eye contact. "But I'm still here to talk about your home life, if you need someone."

Starla's been thinking. It's obvious Hali and Mahr aren't going to tell her where her parents are, or what happened to the rest of her family on Silk Station and to the crew of the *Nanshe*. Not until they get some answers of their own.

She's considered trying to act feral — she's read about feral children, raised away from society, raised without parents; she thinks maybe that's what Hali wants to hear. Poor thing, can you imagine, raised in a situation like that? And deaf no less. It's a blessing we got her away . . .

"How often did you travel with your parents on the *Nanshe*?"

Starla blinks. It takes her a moment to process Hali's signs; she hasn't been paying attention.

"Never." Not since she could barely walk, and they'd brought her here to New Sarjun. But she doesn't remember that, not more than flashes.

"But you were rescued onboard the *Nanshe*."

Starla bridles at that word, *rescued*.

"That was my first time. Training voyage."

"She says it was a training voyage," Hali repeats aloud to Mahr. "Her first time on the ship."

"So she was training to be part of the crew?" Mahr asks.

Starla waits to answer until Hali's interpreted the question. She doesn't want to let on how much she's able to understand. Nor does she trust herself to get all the context without Hali's help, and she doesn't want them to start thinking they can just yell at her and be understood.

"Not crew," Starla answers, and Hali looks satisfied as she repeats Starla's answer for Mahr. "Just training."

She's decided to play the innocent card for now — not the feral card, not the abuse card; she'd never forgive herself for that — but maybe she can distance herself from the more anti-Alliance actions of her parents and the *Nanshe*.

"Did your parents ever talk to you about their trips?"

Starla senses a landmine here. Probes at it. "Their trips?"

"Did they talk to you about what they did when they — " Hali fumbles in her signs, here, thinking. "About where they went on the *Nanshe*? Either before, or after?"

Starla seizes on the last, sensing a distinction she can take advantage of. "Sometimes after. Never before." Again, Hali looks satisfied, and Starla takes a deep breath. "They liked to talk about the places they visited. They would bring me presents."

Hali is repeating Starla's sentences as Starla signs them, and a tension flinches around the room at the last. Starla feels a spike of panic. Presents. Not all of them purchased — and even those that were purchased were certainly not with legitimately earned credits.

She remembers the last gift they brought home from a trip to New Sarjun. Here. Before, Starla had always thought it sounded exotic, but now she wonders how her parents could stand to visit such a horrible place.

It had been at breakfast, a week before that last day.

Raj Dusai was already wearing his shipping-out clothes. The crew of the *Nanshe* didn't have a uniform as such, just a pewter-gray jumpsuit with twin stripes across the chest in some sort of glossy black biofabric that glimmered whenever the crewmember was aboard the ship. Raj was wearing the jumpsuit with his many-pocketed flight jacket and a pair of yellowing white socks that looked out of place. His gravity boots sat beside the door.

He wouldn't wear those on the station, of course, and there they sat whenever the *Nanshe* was in dock. Starla stared at them, ignoring her father, knowing that their familiar spot by the door would soon be vacant — and he would be gone.

And she would be left behind, again.

Lasadi Dusai came in a moment later, holding a package in her arms.

"Oh, good," she said, in response to whatever Raj had said behind Starla's shoulder. "This is for you, sweetheart," she said to Starla, handing over the package to free up her hands. "We love you," she signed.

The package was wrapped in one of the brightly colored New Sarjunian scarves her mother favored. They were too flashy for Starla, but that never stopped her mother from picking them up and then gifting them to her whenever they'd stopped on New Sarjun. Starla unwrapped it carefully. This one was a livid lime green shot through with turquoise and gold, the pattern feathered out from the center. Her mother waved her hand inside Starla's vision. "Peacock feathers," her mother told her, fingerspelling the bird's name.

The scarf was pretty, but once unwrapped, Starla didn't even notice it slide off her lap to puddle on the floor. Inside was a jumpsuit, just like her father and mother both were wearing. Starla gasped in delight and let the whole mess fall off her lap, leaping up to hug both Raj and Lasadi at once, all awkward angles and knobby elbows. She could go on the training voyage. They were going to give her a chance to join the crew.

Starla blinks. She takes a sip of the water. 1, 4, 9, 16 — She's missed whatever Hali is saying to her now.

"What kinds of presents?" Hali signs and speaks, repeating herself.

Starla shrugs. "Scarves," she signs. "Toys," she signs, because it seems like it'll help them keep thinking of her as a kid even though she hasn't been one for years.

"Did your parents ever discuss politics with you?"

Starla considers this new line of questioning, wary. What does Hali mean, politics? As in, who did they think was going to win the presidential election in Arquelle? Starla wrinkles her brow, not sure.

"Did they ever talk about the Alliance?"

Oh. Politics.

Starla strains to see a clear path to navigate through this one. "Not really," she signs. It's mostly true. Her parents may not like the Alliance but they aren't overly political about it. They keep to themselves. Maybe they target Alliance ships more frequently than those that call Durga's Belt their home, but that was just being neighborly. No one throws a dead rat in their own air recyclers.

"Are you very close with your cousins?"

Now another non sequitur. Starla frowns. "Some of them," she signs. "The ones that are my age. And . . ." She shrugs. "They're cousins," she signs. "I like some of them, I don't like others. Doesn't everybody?"

Hali doesn't answer this. Starla has been given to understand that not everyone has as many cousins as she does, and not everyone lives as closely with them. And that not everyone calls every kid they know who's about their age "cousin." If she's honest, she has to admit that she doesn't actually know which ones are related by blood, and which ones are related by virtue of being part of the family on Silk Station. No one at home cared, and she doesn't care either.

"Do you know Amit Dal?"

Starla gives her a look that says, Of course, I'm not an idiot. Amit is her Auntie Faye's oldest son. Auntie Faye is her mother's sister. He's blood relations for sure.

"Did he ever talk about politics with you?"

Oh, yes, Starla thinks, but does not sign. And now she begins to realize where this is going. Amit has been deeply involved with the OIC — the Organization of Independent Colonies — and he's tried to convince her parents to get involved, as well.

Starla wonders if she should pretend not to know what the OIC is.

She's been thinking too long.

"Did he ever talk about politics with you," Hali signs again.

Starla shakes her head, gives a bemused little shrug. "I'm just his little cousin," she signs.

Mahr barks something at Hali when Hali repeats Starla's words. Hali nods. "I think we're going to talk about this some more tomorrow," Hali says and signs. She gives Starla a smile.

This time, when Starla is taken back to her cell, the lights stay on. She wonders if she's done well today.

She can't tell.

———

Starla lies on her cot staring at the ceiling and wonders if Amit made it. If Auntie Faye made it.

If Mona made it.

She wonders if the Alliance blew up her home because they thought her family sympathetic to the OIC.

They aren't — weren't? — except for Amit and a few of the cousins his age. Her parents despise the Alliance, but it hadn't seemed to be in a political way. More in a predatorial way.

The Indiran Alliance doesn't get out to Durga's Belt so much, anyway, there at the flickering far edge of New Sarjunian space.

Indira and New Sarjun are next-door neighbors, and the only two inhabitable planets in the Durga System. That was the bright point in the sky Starla's ancestors had picked as their most likely seed system over a thousand years ago, and Indira had had the distinction of seeming a more likely choice to support a fragile race. The generation ship, the *Ark Matsya*, was still in orbit over Indira. Starla would love to see it — she can't imagine tech that ancient crossing galaxies — but catching even a whiff of Indiran atmosphere would have been risky business for her parents, and so for her.

The other planet in the system hadn't been colonized until centuries later, when rugged, contrary types who bridled under civilized rule decided to see what sort of living they could eke out on New Sarjun's sun-baked crust. The centuries since had put a polish on New Sarjun's rough edges, but it was far from gleaming.

Indira had been a bickering collection of petty states until a few decades ago. By force or by guile, the diplomats from Arquelle, Indira's largest and most powerful country, had talked the rest of the planet into a treaty.

That would have been all well and good, but the Indiran Alliance, led by Arquelle, wasn't content staying planetside.

Colonies on the Indiran moons were pressured to join next. Then colonies farther out. And that might have been successful, but the planetside alliance on Indira was starting to crumble, and countries who'd been amenable at first got to feeling the wrong end of the deal, feeling over-trampled and misused while Arquelle got stronger and more powerful.

And as the cracks began to show, Arquelle became more insistent that the entire Durga System join the Alliance, stretching fingers out to New Sarjun and into Durga's Belt, the asteroid chain just beyond, a rat's nest of unaffiliated asteroid stations and colonies that Arquelle insisted should be registered and taxed. Arquelle and New Sarjun butted heads more than once about that, while most out in Durga's Belt merely scoffed and ignored Arquellian tariffs.

And those who didn't scoff? Like Amit? They joined the Organization of Independent Colonies, and started planting bombs.

Starla had gotten most of her gossip about Amit from Mona.

Mona was like a sugar cube set in a spilled pool of tea, soaking up every drop of scandal until she was full and bursting, then running to Starla desperate to spill everything she'd heard to the one person she could count on not having overheard it all first.

Starla found glimpses into this world fascinating. She'd mastered the world she experienced immediately, and was passing knowledgeable about the world she was taught about on TUTOR. But although her family, most of them, had no difficulty communicating with her, she couldn't overhear the sharp words her aunts and uncles exchanged, the slipped secrets older cousins forgot to keep closed-lipped.

Mona gave her a glimpse into this intriguing silence, flipping salacious signs from her lithe fingers, her facial expressions and posture so perfect that Starla always knew exactly who she was mimicking. Scribbled diary conversations, giggling late at night, rapid-fire texts teasing out secrets about the rest of the family —

The family.

Her parents.

Starla doesn't realize she's crying until the water spills from her eye sockets, streaming into her ears. She jams the heels of her hands into her eyes, knowing they must have her on surveillance and ashamed to let them see her weak.

Starla knows she's never going back to Silk Station.

She's on her own, now, just as her parents, wherever they are, are on their own.

She can't sit around forever.

But she can plan.

# 6

## JAANTZEN

"Major Ximena Nayar is perfect," says Toshiyo. She's starting with the positive news, as is her preference, but Jaantzen can tell by her forced optimism there's bad news, too. He glances at Manu, who's watching Toshiyo with over-eager interest. Jaantzen guesses Manu knows what the bad news is.

Jaantzen braces himself and waits.

They're sitting around the conference table in the upper office; Toshiyo pulls up Nayar's file in the center of the table. There's no picture.

Manu leans in. His hair is an electric orange today, glowing against his midnight skin — he's darker even than Jaantzen — and his nails are painted an opalescent sherbet to match. He's been draped in black for weeks, and Jaantzen suspects this return to vividity is in honor of Jaantzen's failure to kill Coeur.

"She's a requisitions officer, stationed at Redrock Prison and overseeing the supplies," says Manu.

"Where's the picture with this file?" Jaantzen asks.

Toshiyo ignores him and swipes to the next page.

"We have reason to suspect she's turnable," says Manu. "She was born here in Bulari, but her father was Arquellian, an officer in the Indiran Alliance stationed on New Sarjun. That gave her dual citizenship, and she eventually joined the Arquellian navy, then the Alliance forces. Because she was born here she's primarily been stationed on-planet, though she's seen combat, too." Manu scrolls down. "Most notably the slaughter at Teguça. After that, she put in for a transfer back to New Sarjun. She took a command cut to take her current position, though she's retained her rank and security clearance. This suggests that Teguça soured her for fighting."

"And according to my contact at Redrock Prison, it soured her against the Alliance," says Toshiyo. "She's not bold about it, of course."

"High enough rank and clearance status that she can command even the prison warden," Manu says, "and enough connection within the prison that she can pull some favors if she needs to. But enough out of the main chain of command that she can act without as much suspicion. We think with the proper persuasion she would help us."

Manu's nodding as he says it, eyes wide and trustworthy like a waiter bobbing his head as he asks if you want dessert.

Jaantzen steeples his hands over his lips, leaning back. "She sounds ideal," he says. He waits for the bad news.

Manu and Toshiyo exchange a look. Toshiyo swipes at the desk, and an image of Ximena Nayar fills the screen.

That rust-colored skin, those high cheekbones and fierce black eyes, and even though she's not smiling in this image, he's certain that once she does he'll see a ferocious flash of gleaming white teeth, that million-mark smile aged by ten years.

"Coeur," Jaantzen says.

Toshiyo clears her throat. "Nayar is Thala Coeur's older sister."

Jaantzen's processing this. "Does she hate her sister as much as I do?"

"They have the same mother, different fathers," says Manu; it's not an answer to Jaantzen's question. "We think she'll work with us."

Jaantzen's staring at that face, marking the differences: it's all steel and grit where Coeur's is elastic and mirthful, but they have the same bones, the same eyes. "And does she hate her sister as much as I do?" he asks again.

Manu clears his throat. "By all accounts, they're friendly," he says.

"Then we're not working with her," Jaantzen says. "What are our other options?"

Manu and Toshiyo share a look. "They're slim, boss," Toshiyo finally says. Her nails click against the desk keyboard and another three files show up, replacing Ximena Nayar's face. "Gia's still friendly with some of the guards from when she did time there, but none that have maximum security clearance."

Jaantzen scrolls through the guards' profiles, frowning. They may come in handy, but none have the clout they'll need to pull off either a release or a rescue. He's never bothered to cultivate a relationship with anyone at the Alliance prison colonies. He assumed he'd never need it. He'll die before he ends up there, and if he's smart he'll be able to protect his people, too.

As Raj and Lasadi should have been able to do.

Jaantzen remembers laughing over wine with Raj and Lasadi — and Tae. Talking safety nets and fortresses — "We'll set up a child exchange," Lasadi had said, "We'll let you take her when she's a bratty teenager," and Tae, laughing, "Be careful, we've got two bratty teenagers in training to send your way."

Over the years Jaantzen had understood that the Dusais weren't just networking with business partners outside of Silk Station, they were engineering a safety net for their family to land in should the inevitable come.

Jaantzen hadn't understood, then, that Silk Station wasn't their fortress. Even when Raj had shown him diagrams, the way whole wings were actually spacecraft ready to launch at short warning, the escape pods in every home. The Dusais had never meant to hole up there and fight, they'd meant to scatter to the breeze and land soft as they could.

If Jaantzen had understood, he might have spent more time building safety nets and less time building his fortress, his stronghold, which in the end was so easily pierced.

He may not have understood in time to save his own family, but he can still do something for the Dusai girl.

"Who else?"

It comes out angry, and Toshiyo and Manu both tense up. Toshiyo's fingers are hovering over the keyboard like she's thinking, but he's seen this before, her freeze response triggering at his anger. Some self-preservation technique built up during her indenture, maybe.

He takes a deep breath. "Manu?" he asks to give her time.

"We've learned they have a civilian social worker seeing her. A woman named Hali Fernanz. Tosh?" he says gently.

Toshiyo's fingernails clatter again, and another file appears in the center of the desk, a doughy woman with steel-gray hair in a short, harsh bob.

"We think she's a weak point," says Toshiyo, back in the rhythm. Jaantzen takes a deep breath. "She's got a spotless record, and by all accounts seems to be a good advocate for children in the Alliance's prison systems. I doubt she'll do anything illegal, but she seems the type who won't want to see a girl locked up for her parents' crimes."

Jaantzen nods slowly. A woman like that could be useful, but her conscience makes her slippery. It's much easier to work with someone whose loyalty he can buy.

"The officer in charge is Lieutenant Mahr," adds Manu, and Toshiyo flicks Mahr's profile onto the screen. "Reassigned to Redrock Prison seven years ago after misconduct charges in the regular Alliance forces."

"What did she do?"

Manu shrugs.

"I haven't been able to break the classification around that yet," says Toshiyo. "But I did find something else. I broke into her bank accounts on a whim, and the Alliance isn't the only one giving her a paycheck."

"Who else?"

"I'm not sure," Toshiyo says, obviously annoyed by her inability to give him an answer to that. "I've got a trace out on the account, hasn't turned anything up yet. Too many layers. But it's always the same amount: five thousand marks. And it's irregular. Every few months or so."

Jaantzen is intrigued. "What service is our Lieutenant Mahr performing for a mystery party every few months?" he asks. "Can you cross-reference that with records at the prison and see if anything comes up?"

"Already did it, boss." It's why she's worth every penny he's spent on her — her and her arcane equipment.

Toshiyo pulls up yet another screen. "There's a couple things that match," she says, drawing up the highlights as she talks. Manu leans in, curious — apparently they haven't discussed this yet. "There's four deposits. Three match with the prison's grain shipment, and two match with interdepartmental sensitivity training seminars, but I'm guessing both of those are pure coincidence. Because all four match with this."

She pulls up another screen and Jaantzen leans in, deciphering the list of names. "Death records," he says, and Toshiyo nods. She's highlighted four, each of them one day after the date of a deposit into Mahr's account. Each of them listing the cause of death as "Unknown." They are the only four records to do that in an otherwise well-documented list.

Something else about the four gives Jaantzen pause. All are juveniles.

"Inmates who die at Redrock Prison are cremated," Toshiyo says. "But these four are missing cremation records. And" — she swipes at the screen with a flourish, her excitement bubbling over — "I checked into the prison undertaker's bank account."

Four dates are highlighted. Four transfers of one thousand marks each.

"Who's buying these kids?" Jaantzen asks.

"Working on it, boss."

Jaantzen nods. "Is there anything else?" Toshiyo and Manu both shake their heads, glancing at each other for confirmation. "Good work. Figure out how we use this thing with Mahr, and keep at the social worker. She seems useful, but I want to make sure we're solid before we approach her."

Jaantzen stands, buttons his coat. He'll go for a walk, try to make sense of all this. Something here is tickling the back of his brain, and if he can just clear his head he'll understand it.

"Boss, what about Ximena Nayar?" Manu asks.

"Find me more options," Jaantzen says, and he sees the flash of frustration in Manu's face.

He doesn't care. He will not be negotiating with Blackheart's sister.

# 7

## STARLA

Starla wakes in the morning and does squats, ten of them before she sits with a gravity-heavy thud back on the cot. Only two full push-ups before her arms give out.

She tries to remember all the resistance exercises her mother tried to get her to do back on Silk Station, and comes up with tricep dips off the edge of the cot. She manages three.

Jumping jacks: fifteen.

Sit-ups: six.

Starla collapses panting on the cot until she's caught her breath, then does the whole routine again.

She's been picked up and slammed back down, shoved into restraints, marched down hallways at will, and she's done with it.

After today, she's never going to be weak again.

She's made it five rounds and her muscles are shaking with the effort when she finally slumps back on the cot.

Starla knows that Hali believes her. She's not sure what Mahr, that pinch-faced dirt-kisser, thinks, but she's certain that if the Alliance allowed fifteen-year-old girls to be tried as enemy combatants automatically, Mahr wouldn't be bothering with any of this.

She's starting to feel safe. It's time to push her boundaries.

It's time to try for a weapon.

She has no possible weapon but the afternoon cleaning bot. It shocked her, last time she tried to capture it, but today she has a plan. She's been running scenarios in her mind all night, riffing on things Deyva taught her about electronics, about dirty fighting. About making weapons with whatever was at hand.

Deyva.

She hopes he made it out of the station alive.

He was the only one who would teach her anything, at first. She'd been ten years old, swarming the hallways of Silk Station with the rest of her cousins, that day he yelled into the melee that he needed a volunteer.

It was standard that passing mechanics would pluck a kid or two from their games whenever they needed someone small enough to squirm inside the ventilation ducts and smart enough to thread the right color wire. Starla's hand always went up first, even though her lipreading as a child was abominable and she often had no idea what would be required of her. She only knew she could do it.

And Deyva, the first mechanic who, finally, picked her, soon learned it.

Deyva was stocky — he hadn't been born on-station — with deep bronze skin and eyes shining like the brightest stars.

"You," he said, finger pointed at the top of her head, past the others. "What's your name?"

"Starla," Starla said, and was annoyed when she saw Mona repeat it for him.

He said something else, face turned so she couldn't see his lips, and Mona answered, speaking and signing both so Starla could see. "She can't hear you, but I can interpret."

Deyva shrugged, pointed his index fingers at both girls, and jerked his thumbs for them to follow.

Deyva didn't need to talk much, Starla learned over the years. He preferred machines to chatter, and he had a concise way of explaining things that didn't require half the words other people seemed to need. He never tried to learn USL, just developed his own system of nonsense signs that always made the same perfect, economical sense as his explanations.

It was to his bench in the engineering station that she'd disappear whenever she was fighting with her parents, or shirking her lessons with TUTOR, or just bored. Her parents must've suspected where she went — for all she knew, Deyva probably told them — but they never came looking for her there.

She and Deyva hadn't talked much about his past, but she knew it had been quite different from life on Silk Station; he always seemed bemused by the gaggles of cousins and the complete lack of supervision. He had grown up on New Sarjun, she knew, in the capital city of Bulari, and she got the impression that he'd grown up on the streets, like in the entertainment vids she and Mona watched sometimes about the city's crime bosses and gangsters. He had snake tattoos on the backs of his wrists, and a wicked-looking scar on his cheek. When she asked about it once, Deyva just laughed, as he always did. "Kids do stupid things sometimes," he said.

She'd asked her father about it, too, but he provided no more insight. "Deyva's story is his own to tell," her father had said. "But you aren't going to find many out here in the black who like talking about the past."

Starla doesn't think Deyva was just fond of snakes. He has — had? — an OIC tattoo, too. Her parents might not have wanted to talk about him, but as usual Mona was a fount of snooped information, gossiping, during their frequent sleepovers, long after either of their parents had gone to bed.

"He was in the OIC." Mona'd signed the last letters in her lap, low and secret. "On the run from the Alliance."

The official sign for the Alliance is two clasped hands, but between them the girls had used their own sign, cast harshly down to the side with disdain, like a rotted piece of fruit.

Starla reminds herself not to use that one in front of Hali.

Now Starla's watching the cleaning bot's hatch, afraid she'll miss it if she doesn't keep her eyes peeled.

She has no idea what time it is, but she hasn't seen it yet today, and so she tells herself it must be coming soon. She has her blanket clenched in her fists — she doesn't know why they bothered to give her a blanket when it's so horribly hot here — and she hopes that the insulation from it will keep the cleaning bot from shocking her too badly. She has the flimsy water bottle, which no one seemed to care if she kept. She's not sure what she'll do with that, but it seemed wasteful to pass up the opportunity to try something.

After what seems like ages, the little door slides open and the cleaning bot scurries out.

Starla knows from watching it for the last few days that it will make a sweep of the floor clockwise before scuttling up to do a quick swipe of the toilet seat and hopping down to disappear back into the wall. It hasn't seemed to be programmed to notice her movements, as though its makers assumed its electric shock would be enough protection.

And maybe it will be. Starla will find out.

She tenses, launches herself with squat-tired thighs across the room as it scurries onto the seat of the toilet, her blanket folded in front of her like a shield.

Her plan works — she knocks the miniature robot into the bowl, where she expects it to short-circuit in the shallow water. It's not ideal, but she'd rather have the metal parts than the electronics.

It doesn't short-circuit.

The cleaning bot explodes beneath her hands, throwing her back against the wall with a force that seems completely impossible for such a tiny little machine. She thinks she must have screamed.

The synthetic blanket ignites with a rush of heat that she can feel on her cheeks. She flings it away from her; smoke roils off it to pool on the ceiling.

The cleaning bot scurries out of the toilet and escapes through its hatch, trailing sparks.

Smoke chokes the room, and Starla's lungs are burning. Where are the fire-suppressant foams? There's water in the little plastic bottle, still, and Starla flings it in a spray at the blanket, sending up clouds of steam with the black, toxic smoke. She turns away to pound at the door, shielding her stinging eyes.

The door slides open and Starla falls through, retching, into the arms of her two guards. They immediately wrench her singed hands behind her and into cuffs.

Busted.

# 8

---

## JAANTZEN

"It seems you have a problem with directions," Jaantzen says. "And I'm not sure how to make this point to you any more clearly."

The whites of the skinny rat thug's eyes are splashed with red — not anything Jaantzen or his enforcer, Kobe, did to him, but something he did to himself by dipping too frequently into the stash of shard he's been peddling in the southern reaches of Jaantzen's territory. The skinny rat thug's eyes are bulging with fear. As they should be.

Willem Jaantzen is getting back to work. Rolling his sleeves up. Taking the bull by the horns.

It should feel good, yet crackling at the edges of everything he does is the tentative, crystalline sense of a world just on the verge of breaking.

He's used to living in a world of sudden shifts and changes, but this feels different. Off kilter. It makes him want to move cautiously.

He can sense it in his crew: an inability to focus on priorities, a lack of decision and dexterity.

He doesn't blame them — none of them know what they'll be able to expect tomorrow. When he made his plans for Coeur, a period of transience had been set in motion. Now his entire crew — and he himself — are caught in that moment. Caught midway between coming and going, between living and dying.

None of them know if they can relax back into the roles they once had.

"This is the third time I've heard about you selling shard in my neighborhood," Jaantzen says. He picks up one of the blister packs off the table, holds it up to the light. Inside, a waffled black tab coated with white powder: slip it under your tongue and press down, and the waffle-like razors slice through the delicate skin to wash the drug directly into your bloodstream without a physical trace. Jaantzen turns it in his hand; the powder glimmers in the light.

The thug's gaze follows Jaantzen's hand, hungry.

"Who are you working for?" Jaantzen asks.

Kobe cracks his knuckles, a smile creeping onto his boxer's face as he senses a moment of action. The shard-pusher whimpers.

They're in a warehouse south of the Port of Bulari, an area no one bothers to police these days. Honestly there's not much need. For the last few years Jaantzen and his crew have had the area on lockdown, and the neighborhood's improved quite a bit. Restaurants stay open later now. The city buses have stopped routing around it. Real estate values are rising, thank you very much.

He's fended off an incursion or two from Sendera Dathúil, and he stays vigilant against scum like the pusher he's got chained to this chair.

Scum like this have been getting bolder lately, though, and it's only a matter of time before the bigger of the second-tier gangs start testing the seals. No rumors of Jaantzen's vendetta against Coeur seem to have gotten out, but jackals still scent death in the air.

It's what Julieta Yang is worried about.

"I ain't working for no one," the pusher says.

Jaantzen nods to Kobe, and the big man's fist drives into the pusher's stomach. "Where are you getting your supply?" Jaantzen asks. The man chokes on a cough in response. Kobe hits him again.

Jaantzen folds his arms, frowning. "I guarantee whoever keeps you supplied with shard isn't paying you nearly enough for your loyalty," he says. "Kobe — " His comm buzzes: Toshiyo. "Please excuse me for a moment," he says, and he turns away from the mess to answer.

Toshiyo clears her throat. "Boss, we have a problem."

Jaantzen glances over his shoulder, motions for Kobe to continue without him. Always more problems. "Go ahead."

"I put an alert on the lieutenant's account," says Toshiyo. "I wanted to make sure we were the first to know if she had any other big transfers."

The warehouse suddenly seems very cold. "And I take it she has."

"Yeah, boss." He can hear her typing. "And there's more. I finally traced the owner of the account. It's Sendera Dathúil."

Jaantzen takes a sharp breath. Sendera Dathúil is the second largest of the crime syndicates in Bulari, having taken over many of Blackheart's seedier operations when she took her talents into politics. They check off many of the more mundane categories of crime — protection rackets, smuggling, drugs — but they're also rumored to dabble in darker places, like kidnapping street kids to sell as illegal indentures to the mining corporations.

If they're buying kids from the Alliance prison, it isn't as a charity project.

"We have no way of knowing if the money transfer is for the Dusai girl," Toshiyo says, breaking into his thoughts.

That's true, but it doesn't matter. "I'm not interested in learning that the hard way," he says. He turns back to Kobe. "Finish up here, then I'll see you back at home." Kobe gives him a bloody thumbs-up.

"Toshiyo, please coordinate a phone call between myself and Major Nayar."

---

Willem Jaantzen schools his face to business-like, eases the tension out of his shoulders and jaw. Resists the split-second urge to put a bullet through the screen.

"Major Nayar. It's a pleasure to make your acquaintance."

Jaantzen gives her a brief smile.

Ximena Nayar inclines her head, not agreeing, not disagreeing. Watching,

Jaantzen revises his estimation of her. She lacks her sister's aggressive charisma, and if ever she does smile, it won't be her sister's million-mark grin. Nayar has a certain seriousness about her — a certain trustworthiness — that Coeur couldn't mimic if she tried.

She hasn't yet spoken, but Jaantzen is considering doing business. He reads people quickly; he's had to, to survive for so long.

"I don't just help out with jailbreaks," Nayar says flatly. Another woman who despises small talk. She's sizing him up, too, frowning slightly at what she sees.

"Yet you agreed to speak with me," Jaantzen says.

"Curiosity," says Nayar. She doesn't elaborate. Jaantzen assumes this is her way of asking what he wants.

"Starla Dusai," he says. "She's being held at Redrock, and I need to get her out."

Nayar reaches out to tap at another screen; her gaze flickers back and forth as she reads. "Starla Dusai," she says. "Is this political? Business? Leverage?" She looks up. "What's in it for you?"

"The girl's my goddaughter," Jaantzen says.

A subtle shift in the way she's watching him, just for a moment, then her attention moves back to the other screen.

"She's being held in isolation in maximum security, which means they haven't figured out what to do with her yet," Nayar says after a minute. She frowns. "But it doesn't look like she'll stay that way for long."

"Stay what way for long?"

"In isolation." Nayar doesn't look pleased. "A girl that young, they shouldn't be putting her in with the general population. Not in max." A tiny line appears between her eyebrows as she swipes at the screen. "It looks like they've ID'd her as OIC. She'll be treated as an enemy combatant."

Jaantzen bites back a curse. He should have swallowed his pride faster. "Is she in max now?"

"Not yet," says Nayar. "But the move will probably be soon."

"What about her parents?" Jaantzen asks. "Are they in max, too?"

Nayar taps a few more buttons on her screen, and he sees it in her face before she even speaks. "Raj and Lasadi Dusai were killed during the attack on the *Nanshe*," she says.

It's officially gone, now, that clinging hope that the girl would be fine without his intervention, that Raj and Lasadi wouldn't need him to play his part in their safety nets.

The girl has no one, now. No one but him.

Jaantzen takes a deep breath.

"There's something else," he says. "I have reason to believe that the officer in charge of Starla Dusai has been selling juvenile inmates to Sendera Dathúil. My people detected a large sum of money transferred into the officer's account this morning. I worry that the girl is in immediate danger."

Nayar's attention shifts back to her other screen, pulling up information. "Mahr," she says, and her tone of voice says it all. "Always thought that woman was shit."

"I can get you evidence, in exchange for your help with the girl."

Nayar scowls. "Said I thought Mahr was shit. I didn't say I cared."

"It would be quite the coup for you to take her down," Jaantzen says.

Nayar's full attention is back on him, coal-black eyes evaluating and serious. "I think you're mistaken, Mr. Jaantzen," she says. "I don't care what Mahr does. I'm not looking for a feather in my cap. If you come out here and I help you with the girl, I name my price."

"And what is that price?" But he knows it already, he can sense it.

"I'm fully aware of your vendetta against my sister, Mr. Jaantzen," she says. "I want you to promise her safety."

Silence. Jaantzen has been preparing for this moment, for this request, he's told himself he'll do what it takes — the answer will not release his tongue.

"I'll call back," he says instead. "Fifteen minutes."

Nayar nods. She cuts the feed.

Willem Jaantzen's hands are shaking with rage.

---

A cup of green tea. Sitting in his room with the lamps off, the glittering night constellations of Bulari's skyline illuminating the space. A faux-leather couch, expensive and comfortable. A triptych of paintings by his favorite artist hanging above the dining table; Tae bought them for him the week before she died, they stab at his heart every time he looks at them, but he can't bring himself to take them down.

Jaantzen sips the tea; it's too hot, it scalds his tongue. He barely notices.

"Call Julieta Yang," he tells his comm, and it's only seconds before she picks up.

"Willem?" She's been waiting for him.

"Did you know that Raj and Lasadi were dead before you called me?" he asks. No small talk for Julieta.

"Yes." The reply comes immediately, and without explanation.

Jaantzen doesn't need one. Her aim had never been to save the Dusais; she had never cared about the girl. All along she's been worried about the balance of power in Bulari's underworld, should he kill Coeur.

Jaantzen isn't surprised, but he's startled to find himself wounded nonetheless.

"What are you going to do about the girl?" she asks.

"I'm not sure," he says, but it's not true; if he's honest with himself, he's already made his decision. He made promises to Raj and Lasadi that he'd take care of their daughter if anything happened to them, and he made promises to himself that he would have his revenge.

Since meeting Tae, his promises to others have always taken precedent over those made to himself. Killing Coeur went counter to that, but he'd convinced himself it was the right thing to do.

It was time.

He'd fucking earned it.

"What would Tae want you to do?"

The question stings, as she meant it to. "Good-bye, Julieta," Jaantzen says.

He disconnects the line.

---

Jaantzen keeps having this dream, though not as often as he would like. In it, he's sitting at a table by himself in that shady kebab restaurant he frequented in those days, which has the same seasoned soy doner on the rotisserie as every other kebab joint in Bulari — only difference, the garlic sauce at this joint is to die for. He's drinking alone.

It's a time before Toshiyo, before Gia, before Manu, before everyone he works with now.

It's a time when his crew isn't a family — it's a collection of strange characters held together by mutual anger. People he'd grown up with in orphanages, people he knew from the streets. People he trusts only by virtue of the fact that they haven't yet sold him out.

He's alone, until one of the waitresses comes to sit at his table. Thick mud-red hair and skin the rich topaz of a full moon hung low on the horizon. He's startled. They've spoken only briefly; she's never served him. He doesn't come here often, though he's been here more, recently. It feels familiar. He needs somewhere familiar lately.

"You seem lonely." It's a line he's heard from women who want his money, but he doesn't think she means it that way. Something in the way she looks at him is anything but seductive. He can't put a finger on it.

"I've been watching you," she says, matter-of-fact. "And you seem lonely."

Jaantzen smiles politely. It's obvious she doesn't know who he is.

"Tae Boroma." She holds out her hand to him, and the way she does it is so charming, he'd like to give her a false name, see how long this moment could last before she learns he's a monster. But he could never — and already her co-workers are gathering near the pass-through window, stealing glances as if unsure what to do, whether to break in and snatch her away.

"I'm Willem Jaantzen," he says. He doesn't take her hand. He doesn't want to feel the recoil when she realizes her mistake.

"I know," Tae says. The hand stays there, waiting, and finally he shakes it. Her handshake is firm. She smiles. "You wanna get out of here?" she asks, and after too long a moment he finally nods, raises his hand to call over his server.

Tae just shakes her head and stands. "I already got your tab tonight," she says. "C'mon, I got something to show you."

And it's the lights display down by the river, a neutral spot among Bulari's gangs, and she instinctively finds a space for them to sit in the hot New Sarjunian night that's out of the way, safe and secure. She has a flask of cheap whiskey in her bag, but they only take a few sips.

They're still talking when the sun comes up.

---

Jaantzen checks his watch. It's been fifteen minutes, and the tea is finally cool enough to drink without scalding. He takes another sip and calls up a connection with Ximena Nayar. She doesn't greet him, just lifts her chin. In that gesture she looks as fiercely defiant as Coeur in the height of her Blackheart days. He pushes away the thought.

"You have my word," says Jaantzen. "On my honor, all vendetta between myself and your sister is cleared. So long as I return alive and free from Redrock Prison, she no longer has anything to fear from me, or from any member of my organization." He takes a deep breath. "But believe that nothing in the world will save her if you double-cross me."

Ximena Nayar only nods, precise, seeming impatient at his caveats. "How soon can you get here?"

# 9

## STARLA

S tarla figures they'll just put her in another cell, but they only let the smoky air out and toss her back in. The air looks clear now, but it stings her eyes and scours her sinuses.

Starla surveys the damage.

The thin mattress is scorched and soggy on the far end, and the blanket — and her pillow, she notes sourly — are both gone. The brushed aluminum wall above the toilet is licked by a rainbow sheen. The toilet itself is a misshapen hunk of scrap metal now, but somebody's put a bucket out next to it for her to use. Starla wrinkles her nose.

She sits on the damp mattress for a moment, but the smell of scorched metal is giving her visceral flashbacks of the *Nanshe* —

*Strapped in against the maneuvering and helpless while on the screen Silk Station is disintegrating, shuttles and escape pods spiraling away in glittering trails while Alliance torpedoes slice after them, whole wings she never realized are actually parked spacecraft breaking away in fiery cascades, their engines demolishing their berths, the life she knew as a child vanishing before her eyes, the gut-wrenching shudder of the* Nanshe *taking a hit, the acrid, roiling smoke and then the visual panic as the ship is boarded, black-helmeted Alliance soldiers screaming orders —*

Starla squeezes her eyes shut to block out the images, then stands.

She starts another round of exercises — squats, push-ups, jumping jacks. This time with a vengeance.

---

Starla's just fallen back on her cot, too exhausted to care about the singed mattress, when Hali and Mahr enter. Starla pushes herself to sit, frowning.

Hali is looking around the cell, eyes wide with horror. "What happened?" she asks Mahr.

"Your sweet little deaf girl got some big ideas about the cleaning bot," Mahr says — Starla thinks Mahr says.

"Are you all right?" Hali signs and speaks.

Starla nods. She knows the woman means "Are you injured?" and not "Are you still being held in an Alliance prison?"

"What do you want?" Starla asks. She's not in the mood for the Interrogation Twins' stupid questions.

"We want to move you out of isolation," Hali says and signs. Starla glances at Mahr, who seems unhappier than ever, something Starla hadn't thought was possible. When Hali moves again, her speech doesn't quite match her signs. "If you cooperate, you'll be moved to a different wing," say her lips, but her hands say, "It's dangerous for you here."

Starla frowns at that. "Cooperate how?" she signs.

"You're too young to legally be kept here. I can get you assigned to a lower security ward," Hali signs, as she says, "We just have a few more questions about your life on Silk Station."

Starla is grudgingly impressed with her dowdy interpreter. That can't be easy to do.

"What do you want from me?" she asks.

"They need to believe you've been mistreated," Hali signs. "How old were you when your parents first started leaving you behind?" she asks.

Mahr curls her lip. "This is useless," she says.

"She's a troubled child," Hali says. "The Alliance has to take that into account." She turns back to Starla. "We know you don't belong in maximum security prison," she says and signs. "Just cooperate with us."

"And be put where? With my parents?"

Hali falters at this. "I'll see what I can do," she signs

"What did she say?" Mahr's eyes are narrowed — Hali may be smooth in her subterfuge, but she's not a natural liar. Her tension is thickening the air, and Mahr scents it like a jackal.

"She's willing to talk with the child psychologist," Hali says, with a glance at Starla. She has to know Starla can read her lips by this point. "Please, sweetheart," she signs, low and away from Mahr.

"Only if I can see my parents," Starla signs, and Hali's face goes white.

Starla forces herself to stay calm — 1, 4, 9, 16 — and wills Hali to just fucking say it. To just tell her.

"I'll see what I can do," Hali signs and speaks, and Starla pushes herself back against the wall, drawing her knees up between herself and the lie.

"I'm not going anywhere." Starla forces her stiff fingers into the shapes, forces herself not to cry.

Her eyes burn with held-back tears, but she still sees the way Mahr's shoulders relax. She doesn't know why, doesn't care. Hali's trying to say something to her; Starla looks away. She stares at the wall until the Interrogation Twins are gone, then she buries her face in her arms.

---

Hours later, Starla on her singed cot, grieving.

Hali's been lying to her about her parents all along — even if they're still alive, Starla knows now she'll never be reunited with them. Even if she takes Hali's bait, spins horror stories about her tragic, neglected childhood, she'll get the pass back into society alone. Her parents will be executed, or be sentenced to work in Alliance mines, or at the very best rot in this prison forever.

The least she can do is not betray them by giving Hali the poor-little-Starla story she's looking for.

The lights have cycled to night and she's finally beginning to drift off in the near dark when something jolts her awake.

Her door is open, a figure is standing there with arms crossed — she can tell even in the dark that it's Mahr, the way she stands, the angry, angular bent of her hip.

The lights come on, blinding bright now, and Mahr thumbs for Starla to follow her.

Starla sits up, dream-drunk, tear-drunk, confused — what is this? — and holds up a hand to mean *just a minute*.

Mahr shoots her in the chest.

# 10

## JAANTZEN

New Sarjun's northern hemisphere is in summer, and even after sunset it's stifling hot, crackling dry. They've crossed over the desert along with the last light of day, the low sun knifing shadows over the parched sands and highlighting the rims of the craggy canyons with gleaming rays.

Jaantzen has never flown over the desert except once, leaving the planet, and this close-ish proximity to it is at once fascinating and disturbing. It's not a place meant for human habitation; he's grateful to land at Redrock Air Force Base, where he gives the Alliance soldiers fake credentials supplied by Youssef Tabari. Tonight he's Rosco Kudra, CEO of R.K. Refrigeration & Coolants.

Refrigeration and coolants. Jaantzen wonders if it would be an interesting industry to invest in, with the cash he got from dissolving his more illegitimate operations.

Ximena Nayar meets them on the runway. Her handshake is solid and her demeanor trustworthy, but Jaantzen can't stop comparing her to her sister; every gesture and expression conjures up ghosts of Coeur, which in turn conjures up ghosts of Tae. It's a vicious cycle he doesn't need, and he looks away, pretending to take in the security as Nayar explains how this will work.

"Getting her out for questioning shouldn't be a problem," she says. "There's a note in her file already about potential OIC involvement. Sooner or later that means she gets treated like an enemy combatant just to see if we can scare her into spilling anything. The guards won't think twice about a major calling an OIC combatant out for questioning in the middle of the night."

Jaantzen glances back at her. "Would that bother you? If she was involved with the OIC?"

"That's not why we're here," Nayar says, but he can tell the answer is no. Interesting. An Alliance officer sympathetic to the OIC? Toshiyo has found a goldmine in this woman. He makes a note to buy Toshiyo another fancy gadget when he gets home.

He's brought one of Gia's meditech prodigies with him, a lanky boy with a shock of red hair and a complexion wholly unsuitable for New Sarjun; Jaantzen's never seen him without a sunburn. Gia's assured Jaantzen that the boy is her best; Jaantzen never really trusts anyone but her, not when emergency medical aid could be needed. But bringing Gia — an ex-resident of Redrock Prison's maximum security ward — through a possible Alliance checkpoint posed too many risks. The boy, who'll wait with the pilot back at the plane, will have to do.

Jaantzen's going in alone with Ximena Nayar.

The prison sprawls out in front of them a few kilometers from the base, a collection of low brick-and-steel buildings, their roofs slick with solar arrays. There's a fence stretching out between the prison complex and the air force base — no one wants escapees thinking they can hijack an Alliance Air Force plane — but it doesn't surround the complex.

Security is next to nothing apart from a checkpoint in the fence; he's surprised. "Where would you go if you escaped?" Nayar says with a shrug. She's driving a rugged personnel transport with a closed cargo compartment just big enough for a person to fold herself up into; she swerves absently around a familiar pothole. "There's nothing else up here — and no one's crossing that desert on foot."

They park far from the main entrance, near a loading dock that's stenciled with the number 16. "There's a surveillance gap here," Nayar says as she backs the jeep up to it. "Camera's out. I've actually been bitching about it for the last six months since this is my main loading dock for max security kitchen deliveries, but nobody's bothered to do anything." She shrugs. "Might as well take advantage."

Nayar shows her credentials to no one as they enter the prison's main office building, though she exchanges words with the guard — Patch, she calls him — in the control room. He barely looks up from his computer monitor as she tells him she's showing around a vendor.

"I also need to see one of the prisoners," she says, and he does look up at this; Jaantzen tenses. But the guard's broad face shows only brief annoyance, not suspicion. He'd hoped for an obligation-free graveyard shift, apparently.

"Starla Dusai," she says, spelling out the name as he hunts-and-pecks it into the computer.

"Got her," he says. "Where do you want her?"

"Is Interrogation Room 3 available?" Nayar asks. "Good. Set her up there and ping me when she's ready to go. I'm going to show Mr. Kudra around the commissary, but I'll want to see her as soon as I'm done."

The guard's attention flickers to Jaantzen, but only briefly. This must not be out of order, either.

The guard keys them through, into the prison. "This is the general-population facility," Nayar says when they're out of earshot. "Low-risk prisoners only in this building. A lot of them work here, too, in the kitchen or whatever. Reduces the cost of running the place. My main head of purchasing is an inmate. You'll be working directly with him if you sign on."

Jaantzen's half-listening to the patter, picking out the parts that seem relevant and ignoring the parts she'd be telling a potential vendor. She's giving him an actual tour, he realizes, talking about supply chains and fulfillment processes, the electricity usage rates of their current refrigeration systems, and Jaantzen keeps thinking it's taking too long. Shouldn't they have gotten the call by now?

Nayar must have been able to sense his unease. She checks her comm, like she could have missed the guard's message, slips it back in her pocket and keeps talking.

They're as far as the storehouses when he can't take it anymore. "This is taking too long," he finally says, breaking into her tour patter. "Something's wrong."

She doesn't answer, just dials up a number. "Patch, I'm wrapping up here. What's with the girl?"

She's listening, and though her stony expression doesn't change, Jaantzen can read the problem in the tiny flare of her nostrils, the twitch in her jaw.

"The girl's not in her room," she says, switching off the comm. "We need to go."

# 11

## STARLA

Starla falls hard onto ribs and joints already aching from the hellish gravity, the wind *whooshes* out of her lungs. She gasps for breath while footsteps march away, the vibrations getting fainter then stopping abruptly. Whatever Mahr shot her with makes her chest burn like hell.

Starla rolls onto her side, forcing her eyes open to see two uniforms walking away down what looks like an alley between two buildings. They're not the guards who took her to the interrogation room the past few days. Different ones. Mahr's bony hip casts a shadow across the asphalt from the mouth of the alley.

Mahr's talking to someone else Starla doesn't recognize, someone skinny, scruff-faced. Not in an Alliance uniform. The man is gesturing at Mahr as he speaks, but it's just random, punctuative. Unhelpful. Starla gets nothing, except he doesn't seem too happy.

The ground vibrates occasionally in long slow growls — fade in, fade out — that Starla would have guessed were vehicles going by except that there's a pattern to it. Two long, one short. It reminds her of something, she can't figure out what; her head feels like it's stuffed with fiberfill.

When she realizes no one's really watching her, she risks raising her head to look around.

No one's watching her, but there's also nowhere to go.

The alley dead-ends behind her. There's a ladder at the end, but Starla's not strong enough to climb it as fast as she'd need to, to get out of range of Mahr's stun weapon.

Or the other, much more deadly looking weapons carried by the other guards.

Beyond the guards, the alley opens up into a vast paved lot with nowhere to hide; she can just see a fence beyond. Starla fights to keep herself calm. Now isn't the time to panic. Now she needs to figure out what to do.

A change in the vibrations in the ground — it's a vehicle approaching, a van backing into the mouth of the alley. She acts groggy when they come back for her. It's not hard; she's exhausted from the stunner Mahr zapped her with. Mahr barely looks at her, she's still talking with the scruff-faced man. He's sleeveless in the heat, ink scrawled up his scrawny forearms in a pattern that reminds her of Deyva and his snakes.

She can smell his cologne, mingling with baked asphalt and engine oil.

Her heart's racing. She wills herself to stay calm.

Now that they're at the mouth of the alley, she can see that the pavement stretches out beyond the van, see the buildings on either side, lined with loading docks, parked trucks, cargo containers. The inside of the van is smooth molded plastic with no doors.

Once she's inside, she'll have no more options. If she runs now, she might be able to find cover long enough to evade them.

Maybe.

Just as the two guards hoist her to the back of the van, Starla twists in their grip, kicks with all her might towards the left, aiming for the man's groin. Her bare heel connects and the guard drops her, toppling the other guard off balance.

Starla's expecting this; the other guard is not. She lands and drives her elbow up into the soft spot below his sternum as he falls.

She's panting, but she scrambles free, risking only a split-second glance over her shoulder to see Mahr and the scruff-faced man shaking off their surprise.

She runs as fast as she can.

# 12

## JAANTZEN

"You've got to be shitting me."

Nayar is raging at the guard, Patch. Jaantzen's glad to be on this side of the desk.

"You don't know where she is? Who's been in charge of her questioning?" she asks, as though she doesn't already know. She's reading over his shoulder as he pulls up that information. "Alert Lieutenant Mahr that she's missing," she says.

Patch nods, grateful for something to do. He's braced against the brunt of her anger, shoulders tense and jaw clenched.

"She's not answering," he says.

"It's late," Nayar says. "Try again."

"She always answers," the guard says, but he tries again.

"Trace her comm. Is she in her quarters?"

Patch shakes his head. "Her comm's off."

Jaantzen can see the brief moment of thought, flashing through Nayar's eyes. "Keep trying to trace her, and tell me what you find," she tells Patch. "Come with me," she says to Jaantzen, which gets him a slightly longer look from the guard than before. Jaantzen gives the man his most innocuous Rosco Kudra smile.

"Yes, Major," Patch says after a moment's hesitation. "Should I put the base on alert to find the girl?"

"Not yet," Nayar says. "I'll call you if we need backup."

Patch glances back and forth between Nayar and Jaantzen. Jaantzen can see it in his eyes when he decides it's above his pay grade and security clearance to wonder why a refrigeration and coolants executive is joining Major Nayar in the hunt for a teenage OIC terrorist.

"I'll let you know what I find out," Patch says, settling back into his chair.

---

"If I was going to try to offload human cargo in the middle of the night, and didn't already know about the faulty security camera on Dock 16, I'd use the area by the generator building," says Nayar. She's jogging comfortably; Jaantzen is struggling not to pant. "There's an alley there that's secluded and fairly unsecured, and close to the max facility." She slows as they reach a corner, checks the safety on her sidearm.

"So you think that's how Mahr's been smuggling out these kids?"

"It seems the most likely. If we get in a sticky spot, feel free to shoot to kill," says Nayar. "Particularly if we're talking about Sendera Dathúil."

"You don't need witnesses to prosecute Mahr for kidnapping?"

Nayar shrugs. "Mahr's not my problem. I don't care if she walks free." She glances at him. "But quieter is better," she says.

They round a corner and there's a van parked by the loading dock, no windows but the driver's compartment. Nayar swears. "That's one of my supply vans," she whispers. Jaantzen can see her scowl in the wan light. "That bitch is using my van."

"You're sure it's not your people?"

"If it is, they're still where they shouldn't be with a van that isn't checked out."

Jaantzen can hear humming coming from the far side of the van, catches the faintest hint of kosh smoke wafting their way. It smells cheap, acrid. He wrinkles his nose, and Nayar nods and pulls out a knife. "Now," she whispers.

She's around the corner of the van before he can react; he hears a strangled gargle and follows to see a man sprawled on his back. His chest is rising shallowly, but he's not conscious. Apparently being head of requisitions isn't all sitting at a desk.

"I'm faster with a gun," Jaantzen says.

"Smarter if nobody sees you anyway," Nayar says. She passes her ID badge over the reader at the rear of the van and there's a faint hiss of pneumatics as the doors open. It's empty, as Jaantzen suspected. He wouldn't be caught standing around waiting if the cargo had already been loaded.

"Help me with this," she says, and together they load the man into the back of the van. He's wearing a guard uniform; Nayar taps her comm over the ID badge and frowns at the name.

"Anyone you know?"

She shakes her head. "He's in maintenance," she says. "Nobody who should have access to a requisitions van."

She shuts the door, makes sure it's locked to her ID badge only. "Now I guess we wait until they bring her out," she says.

# 13

## STARLA

S tarla's crouched on a ledge about ten meters up, panting. She's figured that hiding and thinking will be smarter than running aimlessly. Whatever Mahr is doing, she seems to be trying to fly dark. Starla suspects she'll have at least a few minutes before Mahr decides it's worth alerting the entire prison.

Beyond the buildings there's a huge swath of asphalt and packed gravel, and beyond that she can see what looks like a launchpad and airstrip. A fence stretches out between the two, but it can't go on forever.

To be honest, Starla barely sees the fence. Despite the pressing need to focus and plan, she's having trouble not gawking.

Overhead, the sky is gaping wide, space stations and super-massive cargo haulers tracing lumbering paths between glittering stars. A blue-tinged star hovering just above the horizon can only be Indira — Silk Station isn't close enough to make Indira out so clearly, so she's never seen it in real life before. Beyond everything, the first of New Sarjun's two moons is starting to rise; right now it's just a sliver, shading the black desert landscape blood red.

The whole scene's alive in a way she's never experienced, the gradients of the atmosphere and wisps of clouds and the burst of some distant electrical storm embroidering it with depth and texture.

It's breathtakingly beautiful.

Starla forces her attention back to the task at hand. She's heard stories of this desert prison. She knows that making a run for it isn't an option — there's nowhere out here to run *to*. But she thinks she doesn't have to escape the entire prison in order to survive this night; she just has to escape from Mahr.

And then?

Then she's back to square one. Say she turns herself in. She's still trapped here answering Hali's questions, no way home, no way of knowing what happened to the rest of her family.

Starla crouches, looking past the fence, out over the airfield.

That would be her way out, if she knew how to fly one of those things. She wonders if she could stow away. They'll need to send in supplies, from time to time, and surely not every plane that lands here is Alliance. Surely there's some that aren't so well guarded.

Starla thinks through her options.

Right now they'll probably be searching any plane that leaves — it only makes sense, with a newly escaped prisoner. But a week from now? They'll assume she ran out into the desert and died. That would be her time to try to get past the fence and stow away.

Through the wall against her back she can feel that same rhythmic vibration, two long, one short, and she realizes it reminds her of the generator back on Silk Station. A generator building will be relatively unvisited, she guesses, and full of places to hide. So now all she has to do is figure out how to get inside this building, and then live there for a week.

Starla ignores how absurd this plan sounds.

She might be able to get in through the roof, she thinks, but first she'll have to get onto the roof. The ladder she climbed stops at this ledge.

The ledge, though, wraps around the building to Starla's left. It's narrow and exposed, but she hasn't seen anyone come by yet. She might be able to risk it, if she inches along.

Starla stands, shuffles away from the safety of the ladder. She tries not to look down.

She's never needed to be afraid of heights before.

---

She's trying to move as seamlessly as she can, hoping that translates into silently, and she's just turned the corner when she sees movement. It's one of the guards. Starla freezes; he doesn't look up.

He's walking softly, as though trying to be secretive — and limping, Starla notes with satisfaction. Starla hopes this means she's right about Mahr not calling in reinforcements just yet. He passes right underneath her, and she stays as still as possible, trying not even to breathe until he's out of sight around the corner.

Starla counts to twenty, let that be enough time for him to pass by, then begins her slow shuffle. Now that she's around the corner, she can see another ladder ahead, leading off a small balcony. If she can —

She feels her bare foot hit a loose brick, watches in horror as it skitters along the ledge and plummets to the ground below. Is the guard far enough away? How loud a sound did it make?

Starla shuffles faster along the ledge now, as fast as she can stand, keeping her gaze on the balcony ahead. She's ten meters away. Nine. Eight.

Movement below: the guard has returned to investigate. She's loud now — she must be with how fast she's moving — and he looks up. His face registers shock and he says something, with lips tight and close. Whispering, not yelling. Still trying not to attract attention, she hopes, and she ignores him, keeps moving. She's two meters away from the balcony when he raises his gun.

Starla feels the energy sizzle past her as she makes a final leap, desperately judging the amount of force she needs to bridge the gap.

Her open palms slam against the lowest rail of the balcony — not the top, as she'd been hoping — the grotesque weight of her New Sarjunian body threatening to tear her grip loose. She swings wildly for a terrifying moment, then manages to hook her heel up onto the balcony and pull herself in.

Another bolt of energy sizzles past with a blaze of blue light, leaving a slice of pain along her upper arm in its wake. The small hairs on the back of her neck are standing on end, and she can smell burning. The sleeve of her jumpsuit is scorched, the bricks behind her are cracked and smoking.

Starla has miscalculated. She'd thought they wouldn't kill her. Apparently she'd been wrong.

# 14

## JAANTZEN

J aantzen doesn't like waiting, and something feels wrong in this night. The man in the back of the van, Jaantzen wonders what he'd say if he could be asked — whether he knew who he was waiting for, or if he'd merely been given a routine task with no explanation.

And what if Nayar hadn't wanted him, Jaantzen, to be able to ask anything? The thought whips through his brain like a flash at the corner of his vision: fleeting, yet leaving an uncomfortable smudge of uncertainty in the spot where it had been. He glances over. She's looking out into the darkness, forehead creased in thought.

"How do we know they'll bring the girl here," he says. He doesn't like all this uncertainty. Doesn't like being surrounded by Alliance soldiers. Doesn't like being at the mercy of Coeur's sister.

"We don't," Nayar says. "It's the most logical place, but we have no way of knowing for sure what Mahr's up to." She shrugs. "This is all conjecture."

"I don't like conjecture."

"I imagine not." Her attention has slid off him, though, into the shadows around the buildings. The flat darkness is reverberating with tiny noises: the hiss of ventilation systems kicking on, the slow *WUB-wub-wub* of a generator deep inside one of the buildings.

Nayar moves suddenly, and Jaantzen's hand is on his pistol, aiming it at her head as Nayar's own weapon leaps up to match, a split second too slow for it to have mattered. Her lips break into the ghost of a smile; she pulls up.

Jaantzen slowly lowers his pistol.

"Touchy," she says, sidearm dropping back to ready as she turns away from him. "I'm just here to help. And if you — "

Somewhere, not too far away, the night sizzles with the charge of a plasma carbine set to its maximum. It echoes in the alleyway; to Jaantzen, it sounds like it's coming from every direction at once.

"C'mon," Nayar hisses, and she's sprinting forward, away from the direction they'd come from.

She's nearly out of sight when a figure flashes out from behind a pile of crates, launches itself at her. They roll, grappling. She's strong, but the man's scrappy and tough, all wiry ropes of muscle and street-fighting technique — dodgy and dirty. He's not in uniform, he's just wearing a close-fitting biosilk shirt cut short to show off tattoos, and baggy pants that give his kicks better range. Nayar's military-trained blows aren't landing. Jaantzen catches the glint of a knife the second before it plunges downwards.

Jaantzen fires.

The skinny thug drops to the ground, the knife clattering to the asphalt beside him. Nayar stands, wincing, and kicks the knife away from the man's reach.

But he won't be reaching for anything.

Jaantzen nudges one ropy arm open, sees the familiar Money-Beauty-Death symbols intertwined with nudes on his forearm. "Well, there's your evidence," he says.

"What is?"

Jaantzen stabs a finger at the tattoo. "Sendera Dathúil," he says. "Anyone else caught with this tattoo is killed."

Nayar nods slowly. "Thanks," she says.

Jaantzen's looking around, doesn't see anywhere the familiar clunky shape of the carbine they'd heard. Besides, if this thug'd had one, he'd've probably used it instead of going hand to hand with Nayar.

For a brief moment he wonders if it was a decoy, a lure to get them away from the van so the delivery can finish, but then the sound comes again, twice, and a flash of electric blue reflects off a stack of oil barrels a hundred meters away.

"Let's go," Jaantzen says, breaking into a run.

# 15

## STARLA

Starla searches for a weapon. Sees the cracked bricks where the guard's blast hit, grabs one. Takes careful aim and hurls it — again she miscalculates the force needed, and the brick shatters at his feet. She's rewarded by another blast from his gun — it hits the ladder behind her and energy crackles up the metal tubing. Starla stares at it, wide-eyed, hairs rising on her arm where it's inches away from the metal. Apparently climbing to the top of the building while hoping he doesn't hit her won't be an option.

She throws another brick, deliberately aiming this one at his feet to test the force she'll need, and as it shatters there, he looks up with a cocky grin. He says something to her, his torso jerking in a laugh, and in the second he looks down to check the charge on his gun, she throws a third brick.

True aim, this time. It hits him square in the ear and he nearly drops his weapon, throwing his hand up to the wound. His fingers come away black with blood. He dodges her fourth brick, and Starla flings herself back against the wall as he raises the gun. Part of the balcony crumbles away as he shoots. Starla pulls her feet back from the edge, panic rising as she readies herself for the next shot.

It doesn't come.

She risks a glance, brick in hand.

Mahr is here, now, yelling and waving arms, and obviously furious with the guard. Starla relaxes a fraction. Maybe she'd been right, and the plan wasn't to kill her after all. She watches Mahr yell for a few seconds, then makes her decision.

Starla starts to climb.

Her hands are claws on the rungs, her heart racing with both the effort of the climb and the terror she feels waiting for the blast that will electrify her molecules into the metal.

When it comes, it's not the electric shock she's expecting. Instead, the ladder shudders and shards of brick rain down on her from above; Starla ducks her head and closes her eyes against the ferocious hail. She can feel the metal of the ladder shrieking as it twists under her weight, looks up in horror as the struts attaching it to the brick above pop loose one by one and the ladder slowly peels away from the wall.

Starla tries to climb down, but her feet slip off the rungs as the ladder tips backwards by degrees, faster and faster until it's gone horizontal with a crash against the balcony. The impact breaks the last of her grip.

Starla falls.

# 16

## JAANTZEN

Jaantzen's yelling as the Alliance woman — she can only be Mahr — takes aim at the ragged figure on the ladder. But he's too far away, and his shot skims past her when the charge from her own weapon jolts her out of its path. He ducks for cover as the guard beside her turns and fires. Nayar's ended up on the opposite wall, taking cover behind a stack of crates.

The plasma carbine leaves a smoking black char on the asphalt beside him — apparently the Alliance version of this weapon has gotten a boost beyond what Jaantzen is familiar with. Nayar leans out from cover and fires, but her shot goes wide, and she's rewarded by a charge from the carbine that ignites the contents of the crates she's hiding behind.

Someone is screaming. High above the battle scene. And Jaantzen watches in horror as the lanky teen girl who can only be Starla Dusai clings to the shrieking wreck of a metal access ladder as it rips from the building and twists on itself with a stuttering pop of rivets. The slow fall picks up speed until her grip is torn free and she falls a full story to the ground below.

He fires at where Mahr had just been standing, a second earlier, and hits nothing.

A minor avalanche of crumbling bricks and twisted metal is raining down around the girl. He can't tell if Starla is moving.

He also can't tell where Mahr ducked to hide, but the guard with the plasma gun is in a doorway, and he's raised the weapon to fire at Ximena Nayar once more.

Jaantzen can't get a clear shot from his corner.

He bellows and charges out from hiding, only faintly aware of Nayar following his lead.

The guard pivots, squeezes the trigger, but one of Jaantzen's slugs catches him in the shoulder and it jerks the carbine off target, the blast sizzling past Jaantzen's sleeve with a stench of charred wool. Jaantzen's next slug goes between the guard's eyes.

Searing agony catches Jaantzen in the ribs, left side, and he bites down on the pain, whirls to face Mahr, her hiding place betrayed by the shot she took at him.

Somewhere through the rush of blood in his ears he hears Nayar yelling, and in the split second before he pulls the trigger he hears her and drops his aim from chest to belly.

Lieutenant Mahr falls back against the wall, hands clenched and bloody around her gut.

"I've got her," Nayar says behind him. "Get to the girl."

Jaantzen glances at his comm. An alert from his biosilk chest armor tells him that he's been shot — Thank you, technology — and that he's broken a rib. It also tells him he doesn't seem to be experiencing any internal bleeding. Gia's meditech prodigy back at the plane is getting the same alert. He'll be ready for triage when they get back.

And Starla — her eyes are open and blinking rapidly in shock; she's lying on her back with her leg bent at a sickening angle, but shielded from the largest chunks of debris by the twisted skeleton of the ladder, which is propped above her. A fierce, protective place has opened up in Jaantzen's chest, drowning out the searing stab of pain through his ribs as he flings the debris off her.

Her eyes focus on him and widen in panic, and somewhere in the adrenaline flooding his mind he pulls up a few of the signs Raj taught him the last time Jaantzen met his goddaughter, so long ago.

"Hello, Starla."

He hopes he has her name sign right. "You're going to be safe," he tells her, trying to speak clearly. "You're going to be safe."

The panic in her gaze ebbs slightly, and she doesn't try to fight him as he checks her for injury. The leg seems the worst, and she grunts as she pushes herself up to sit, face a mask of pain. Jaantzen's surprised she hadn't shattered like a stick of hard candy at the fall. She's gaunt, unsubstantial, skin nearly translucent with shock and from growing up in the black.

She signs something to him, and he shakes his head, not sure what she's said. She scowls and jabs at his broad chest, then opens up her hands in question.

In the distance, an alarm is going off. He can hear shouting, getting closer.

"It's time to go," Nayar says behind him. "Can she be moved?"

Jaantzen nods. "I think so," he says to her. "I'm a friend," he says to Starla. She frowns at him, and he's not sure if she's understood. He holds out a hand. "We have to go. You'll be safe."

She takes his hand, and he ignores the pain in his ribs as he hoists her up to stand on her good leg. She cries out in pain.

Behind them, Mahr is still lying against the wall, gasping for breath. Her eyes widen with recognition as he turns, her expression shifting from fear to surprise. "Willem Jaantzen," she says. Her gaze darts back and forth between Jaantzen and Nayar. "Major Nayar, what are you doing with — "

Jaantzen winces at the crack of Nayar's pistol. Mahr slumps back against the wall.

"During a routine tour with a vendor, I came upon the lieutenant in the process of illegally selling an inmate into indenture," she says quietly. "Unfortunately, Lieutenant Mahr resisted arrest. Equally unfortunately, the vendor has chosen not to do business with the Alliance."

She reholsters her pistol. "A shame, but I'll get over it. As for the girl, she ran off in the confusion. I doubt we'll find her — and certainly not alive." Nayar straightens and tosses him the key to the jeep. The shouting is getting closer. "Head back through this alley and take a left to find Dock 16. Keep the girl out of sight, and if anyone at the checkpoint asks, tell them I stayed late to take care of some business."

Her expression is fierce as she takes his offered hand.

"Pleasure doing business with you, Major," he says. "Until next time."

A brief snort of a laugh quirks her lips into an exact image of her sister, but Jaantzen just turns away, arm supporting his goddaughter.

He has family to take care of, too.

# 17

## STARLA

The man who knows her name sign motions for Starla to get into the coffin-like crate in the back of the jeep, and she does, trusting, screwing her eyes shut against the sight of him putting the lid over the top. He's the biggest man Starla has ever seen, tall as her station-born cousins but bulky, too, in a way that's hard to get out in space. His expensive-looking suit is tailored perfectly around his broad shoulders and barrel chest. His skin is a rich, deep brown. Diamonds glitter in his ears.

Something about him feels familiar, she thinks. She's not sure why, but something about this ferocious, gun-toting man feels right.

And he knows her name sign.

The engine of the jeep thrums through her chest, each bump and stutter sending waves of pain and nausea sloshing up from her leg. They stop once, for a long time, and she tries not to panic though she's desperate to know what's going on.

Finally the jeep starts moving again, and a moment later the engine is off and she feels her crate moving, bites her lips, can only hope she's kept herself from screaming out in pain. Feels herself resettled, and then searing light slices through the gap as the lid is removed.

She blinks, pushes herself to sitting. She's *inside*, but she can't tell inside what. Something narrow like a cargo shuttle; there are stacks of crates just like hers strapped against the wall.

The big man is here, too. He pauses, takes a deep breath.

"Hi, Starla," he signs again. It's clumsy, mechanical.

"Who are you?" she asks, but apparently that's it for his bag of sign language tricks. He grimaces, looking embarrassed, and pulls out his comm. Speaks to it — she catches "My name is," she thinks — and passes it to her.

MY NAME IS WILLEM JAANTZEN. I'M A FRIEND OF YOUR FATHER'S, AND I'M HERE TO GET YOU AWAY AND SAFE.

"Where are my parents?" she signs

Starla signs the words frantically, and Willem Jaantzen — she knows that name, her parents had talked about visiting him — furrows his brow, gestures at the comm. She types the question and thrusts it at him.

And then he meets her gaze, his own holding none of the pity that was in Hali's expression, none of the softness or the fear to tell her the truth. Willem Jaantzen's gaze holds nothing but cold anger. "Your parents are dead," he says softly, passing the comm back, but she doesn't need to look at the words blinking there to understand what he said.

Starla isn't surprised, not any more.

"Thank you," she signs, and he nods.

He glances over his shoulder, says something to a smaller, younger man with bright-red hair and a duffel bag. Together, they hoist Starla from the crate and onto a reclined chair with a flight harness, and for a brief moment she thinks they're going home, they're heading back to the stars. But this isn't a shuttle, it can't break the atmosphere, not without tearing itself apart and scattering them across the surface of New Sarjun in a spectacular, fiery hail.

Jaantzen hands her the comm. WE'RE GOING TO MY HOME, it

says. *YOU'LL BE SAFE THERE. THIS IS NOLE, HE'S GOING TO LOOK AT YOUR LEG. IS ANYTHING ELSE INJURED?*

Starla shrugs, staring at the last sentence. Everything aches, but it has for days. And nothing's screaming at her worse than her leg.

Nole's already got scissors out, the metal is cold against her calf as he slits the material of her jumpsuit. Jaantzen reaches across her to snap the harness in place, then sits, wincing, in a seat beside her. She wonders if he's been shot: there's a hole singed in his expensive jacket, but no blood.

Jaantzen shouts something to the pilot and the plane begins to roll, faster, faster, she's pushed back in her seat with the motion, like the *Nanshe* under thrust — like, but not the same. She can feel the moment the wheels peel away from the planet's surface, the smooth glide tilting upwards, with a rush of adrenaline in her gut that's almost euphoric.

She relaxes against the chair, lets her head roll to look out the window. She expects to see stars; instead she sees the second of New Sarjun's moons cresting the horizon in a glimmer of cold fire. It's a view Mona would have loved to see. *Would* love to see.

Starla waves to get Jaantzen's attention, makes the sign for *comm*, which he probably doesn't understand, though he hands her the device.

*NEED TO FIND OUT WHAT HAPPENED TO MY FAMILY.*

His broad brow furrows at that. She can see him wondering if he needs to tell her again what happened to her parents.

*COUSINS. AUNTS. WHOEVER.*

She has to find out if she's alone. She has to learn what happened.

Jaantzen takes back the comm to respond, but his speech is slow and clear. "You have my word."

Starla turns to stare back out the window. The moon has risen fully now, liquid gold flowing over the crumpled-paper landscape of the desert. It's unlike anything she's ever seen: raw, surreal. Stunning.

# DEVIANT FLUX

## STARLA'S STORY IS FAR FROM OVER.

*She thought nothing could come between herself and her new family. She was wrong.*

It's been five years since Starla Dusai's home station was destroyed by the Alliance, and she's spent every minute searching for evidence that she wasn't the only survivor.

When she receives a tip that her beloved cousin Mona is alive and well on an astroid station out in Durga's Belt, she drops everything to find her. Thrust into an unfamiliar world of crime cartels and union politics, Starla soon realizes Mona is caught up in a dangerous plot — and that saving her might just mean giving up the new family she's come to love.

If it doesn't get them both killed first.

jessiekwak.com/deviant-flux

# ACKNOWLEDGMENTS

Sometimes writing seems like a lonely process, but even with a book this short, plenty of people were involved in the making.

First, I want to thank Elly Blue for creating her fabulous feminist bicycle science fiction anthology series, *Bikes in Space* — and particularly for purchasing my short story "Bikes to New Sarjun" for the second anthology. Were it not for your email nudge asking why I hadn't submitted yet, I may never have discovered the Durga System.

Thank you to my husband, Robert Kittilson, for letting me ramble at you for hours upon end about my story problems, and for your often ingenious solutions. I promise I'll put a bike messenger in the next one.

A HUGE thanks to Andrea Rangel and Kathy Kwak for being willing to read my first drafts. To both of you, your feedback is invaluable, and your bluntness is greatly appreciated. Also, mom, thank you for teaching me letters and words and all that good stuff!

Thanks to Jackson Tjota (tjota.daportfolio.com) for the gorgeous cover art and to Fiona Jayde (fionajaydemedia.com) for the cover design. You guys rock!

And, finally, a hundred million high fives to the spectacular Kyra Freestar (Bridge Creek Editing) for your phenomenal editing work on this.

## ABOUT JESSIE KWAK

Jessie Kwak is a freelance writer and novelist living in Portland, Oregon. When she's not working with B2B marketers, you can find her scribbling away on her latest novel, riding her bike to the brew-pub, or sewing something fun.

Learn more about me (and get free books!) by signing up for my mailing list at www.jessiekwak.com.

*Connect with me:*
www.jessiekwak.com
jessie@jessiekwak.com

# THE BULARI SAGA

## A DURGA SYSTEM SERIES

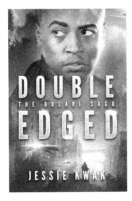

### Book 1: Double Edged

Thala Coeur — Blackheart — is dead. But Willem Jaantzen's relief is short-lived when he realizes she's sent him one last puzzle from beyond the grave. As he and his crew are plunged back into a game he thought they'd left far behind, one thing becomes painfully clear: this secret isn't just worth killing for. It's worth coming back from the dead for.

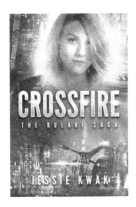

### Book 2: Crossfire

The Bulari underground is back at war, and Willem Jaantzen has the sinking feeling the only way to end it is to betray the people he loves the most. And as his goddaughter, Starla, chips away at a seemingly unrelated mystery, bringing peace back to Bulari is quickly becoming the least of his worries.

Keep an eye out for the rest of the series:

jessiekwak.com/durga-system

# THE DURGA SYSTEM SERIES

## STANDALONE NOVELLAS

Manu Juric is a mediocre bounty hunter. But he's damn good at reading people and creating unexpected explosions — and that can take you a long way in this business.

Just not far enough, he learns when he tries to take out one of Bulari's most notorious crime lords: Willem Jaantzen.

Five years after Starla Dusai's home station was destroyed by the Alliance, she's still searching for evidence that she wasn't the only survivor. When she receives a tip that her beloved cousin Mona is on an astroid station out in Durga's Belt, she drops everything to find her. But Mona is caught up in a dangerous plot — and saving her might just mean Starla giving up her new family. If it doesn't get them both killed first

Find bonus Durga System stories and more:

www.jessiekwak.com/durga-system

# ALSO BY JESSIE KWAK

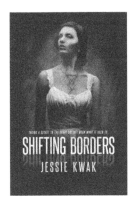

It's been years since the Ramos sisters have been close, but when Patricia is accidentally possessed by Valeria's dead boyfriend, Marco, they have one last shot at working out their differences. But with a drug smuggling gang hot on their heels, will they have time to heal their relationship?

***From Razorgirl Press.***

Worried about the state of business during the zombie apocalypse? You're not alone. This humorous collection of zombie short stories proves that festivity and productivity can still coexist alongside weapons trainings during hard times. It includes pieces previously published in *McSweeney's Internet Tendency*, *Bikes in Space 3* (*Pedal Zombies*), and *Mad Scientist Journal*, along with illustrations by Natalie Metzger.

CPSIA information can be obtained
at www.ICGtesting.com
Printed in the USA
FFHW021028310819
54583165-60274FF